The Assignment

W.G. Walters

Writers Club Press
San Jose New York Lincoln Shanghai

The Assignment

Published by Writers Club Press
an imprint of iUniverse.com, Inc.

For information address:
iUniverse.com, Inc.
620 North 48th Street
Suite 201
Lincoln, NE 68504-3467
www.iuniverse.com

ISBN: 0-595-01035-0

Printed in the United States of America

To those who seek truth.

Acknowledgements

I have so many people to thank for this book. There's my mother, Ann ("And just how much is this going to pay you?"); Art (who kept me up all night so I could write without distraction); Barbara ("So, you're writin', huh?"); Bianca ("Heath told you're getting a poem published?"); Dar ("I think you were meant to be a writer."); Erin ("Wanna work cleaning pipes with acid forty hours a week?"); Heath ("Really? Published? Wow!"); Keeley ("You wrote a book? Coooool!"); Leigh Anne (wide eyes, deep breath); Melissa ("So you wrote a book. When the hell are you going to get a job?"); and Richard ("…"). So many others, also, that cannot possibly all be named.

Chapter One

Doctor Nancy Villareal calmly walked into the briefing room, her cool demeanor hiding her wildly flaying nerves that were usually made of steel. It was the event she had spent her entire life preparing for, dedicating ten years of study in astrophysics to the cause. A perfect set of grades sealed her seat on the long upcoming journey. Now, her certainty and confidence were so great that nothing could persuade her to abandon her lifelong dream.

She stepped to the large, rectangular table in the otherwise empty room and looked over the nameplates. The flight commander and pilot were both experienced astronauts, Captain Rick Newman leading three shuttle missions before his suspension. Most of the other names meant nothing to her, except one that she recognized as belonging to someone she grew up with in New Hampshire. She always had feelings for Joe Rommel, but stayed away from him romantically because of his insanely different beliefs. He had been a strange boy, reading everything he could about anything out of the ordinary and often ignoring other, more important subjects. The last time she had heard anything about him was at their five-year class reunion when she learned he had taken a job in Boston. Perhaps he had straightened out his ways and she could finally admit her feelings to him. If not, it would be a much longer trip than anticipated.

She took her seat next to the pilot's, waiting for the others to arrive. She drifted into a daydream about what they would find. Several minutes later, she was jerked back to reality as Joe walked in with a smile already beaming in her direction. An involuntary giggle came out of her throat as she rose and simply embraced him in a passionate hug he gladly returned. "Joe!" she nearly whispered as they held on to each other. Almost a full minute passed before she let go and looked him over to see that he had been taking good care of himself. She broke the silence first, saying, "It's been so long. How have you been?"

Joe was no slouch when it came to those he still considered friends, as Nancy had seen when a mutual friend of theirs had written to him for help in high school. He had left for a few weeks that summer, but when he returned he said he could not find the person she asked him to look for because he did not know the real name of the man he was looking for. "I'm doing fine," he said. "When I was told you were on this mission, I had to ask several times to make sure it was you." He leaned over to her, as if trying to prevent unseen ears from hearing. "Are you still trying to prove it?"

She slid back into the chair as mixed emotions came over her with the memories of the problems that kept them apart in high school. "Yes," she answered with only a hint of shakiness. She thought it was good compared to what she was afraid it might have sounded like. "I've done everything I said I would to get on this flight, and now here I am. Perseverance pays off."

Joe gave a brief, downbeat chuckle as he walked to the coffee bar and poured some for each of them. She was surprised he remembered her two sugars, and she was happy about it. "Well," he slowly began as he rubbed his curly, brown hair, "I really hate to tell you this, but when we get out there, there may be times when we're in a debate about that."

Dejection worked its way through the emotional turmoil inside Nancy. She was able to conceal it except for her mouth, which moved from a warm smile to an odd smirk as her eyes drifted to the side. "Why is that?" she asked.

A moment passed as a brief look of wonderment crossed her friend's face. It dawned on her that he must still be half-delusional and was trying to figure out the best way to tell her. Either insane or embraced by the demands of the deluded. Ridiculous as it was, he was the one who chose his lifestyle and she had no right trying to force anything on him rather than let the truth speak for itself. He must have been chosen because of what NASA thought they may encounter on this first-of-its-kind assignment.

Joe sighed and took the seat next to her even though it did not have his name in front of it. Taking a glance downward, he said, "This is the first manned deep space mission, so they wanted to take no chances on us running into something we couldn't handle. So they came to me." He paused, and she knew what he would say, though not the exact words. "I have spent the last ten years making a living studying the unknown."

"You study flying saucers," Nancy filled in, her hopes shattered.

Joe chuckled again and responded, "Not usually. Occasionally. I usually stick with things like ghosts, mental powers, crop circles, that sort of thing. But although I've never really dealt with a saucer, I've spent a lot of time studying biology. I'm trying to figure out what alien physiology might be like. I even took a couple of courses at a community college near my home." Nancy was glad that he still did not completely lose touch with reality. "Biology and chemistry, mostly, but a geology course, too. I wrote a couple papers in Paraview magazine that were considered so impressive they were quoted in Scientific American."

The blonde bombshell visibly reacted to this, much to her surprise remembering. "I think I may have heard about that. My thesis advisor mentioned something along those lines." She turned away as she added, "She was mad." It was an understatement. She had written several letters to the magazine and encouraged her students to do so as well. Nancy had sent two. The magazine published one of her advisor's letters. Although the editor's response was well-put, concise, and gentle, it was not what they had been hoping to receive. "So, you're here in case we meet anyone or encounter anything contrary to what I'm trying to prove."

He gave a sad grin. "I'm afraid so."

They both turned to the door as it opened to admit a shorter, plump man with short, dark blond, messy hair in a blue astronaut's outfit like the one they were wearing. "Hello," he said with great tension, "I'm Adam McCrone, the engineer for this mission."

Nancy and Joe rose to their feet as he walked over to them, Joe holding extending his hand to the new arrival. "I'm Joe Rommel, parapsychology expert. This is Nancy Villareal. She's our astrosciences expert. I'm sorry I was in your seat, but we haven't seen each other since our high school graduation."

"How do you do?" asked Nancy as she offered a handshake.

Adam smiled weakly as he timidly as he shook their hands and said, "That's all right. You know we're not coming back, anyway."

"What?" Both of them said at the same time. Nancy knew without looking that Joe's expression was the same as hers.

Joe went to his seat on the other side of the table so Adam could take his. A look of resignation was on the engineer's face as he said, "No, we're not. I'm the only engineer on this mission and it's some new, untested design. It only takes one problem for us to never get back, and we're going to be gone for well over a year."

Before Joe could respond, a tender, mature, British baritone from the door said, "That's not a proper attitude for an engineer, much less an astronaut entrusted to maintain a new engine in flight." They looked over to see a gray-haired man in the same blue outfit strolling into the room. "There's always a chance you can be wrong," he said. "You just have to make sure you know whether you need to be wrong, and how to do it. I'm Doctor Walker Licht." He held out a hand to Joe, the nearest person to him.

As Joe stood and shook the medical officer's hand, he said, "I'm glad to see that the man I'm trusting with my good health for the next year is so positive and can think so clearly. I'm Joe Rommel, parapsychology expert."

"Nancy Villareal, astrosciences," the petite blonde said as she took the offered hand.

Adam hesitantly accepted the grip as well and said, "I'm sorry. I tend to worry a lot. Adam McCrone, engineer."

Doctor Licht smiled warmly and said, "Far, far too many people worry a lot. Many of them get in trouble, but some are able to make something of their life. Since you're here, you must have some level of confidence."

"I hope so," said Adam, making Nancy and Joe glance at each other. How did such a worrywart get selected for such an important mission? "I know that you have the know-how to get all of us back all right. That's good. That's real good."

Still smiling, Doctor Licht turned to Joe. "Mister Rommel, I understand you've had some training in biology. Do you have any medical knowledge?"

The question surprised Nancy, but she felt it should not have; any foreign particle could become a problem to be dealt with by the doctor. "Yes," he said, "I have a basic understanding of the field, but I've been assigned as an expert in xenobiology."

"Xenobiology?" asked the surprised physician. "That's something I wasn't entirely expecting."

Just then, a highly attractive Hispanic brunette joined the group, tall and well endowed. Nancy felt a touch envious. "*Hola*," she said jubilantly with what sounded like a native Mexican accent. "I am Doctor Yolanda Flores. I have been assigned as the science officer on this expedition."

"Walker Licht, Doctor of Medicine."

Nancy's eyes rolled up as she realized how many times she would have to introduce herself. "Doctor Nancy Villareal, astrophysics."

Adam shakily held out his hand, then retracted it, then held it out again as he introduced himself. Doctor Flores quietly nodded with a smile and took the hand.

Joe stepped forward and gave a slight bow of the head with a beaming smile. "Joseph Rommel. My specialty is parapsychology, but I've been assigned for xenobiology." Nancy wondered how many times she would hear that in the next two years.

With a slight tilt of her head to the left, Doctor Flores asked, "What is xenobiology?"

Nancy said a single word. That one word made her feelings on the subject quite clear, but was highly unprofessional. She did not care about the quick looks she received.

After Joe took his glance at Nancy, he said, "To a lot of people it is, but it's actually a very useful field in anthropology. We have yet to see if it will actually ever be needed on our journey." Turning back to Doctor Flores, he explained, "It's the study of previously unknown life forms."

"Oh", said Doctor Flores. "Interesting." The questions in her head were obvious from the pause before she said it and the way her eyes momentarily rolled up into her eyes. Nancy began to think she had an ally on the expedition and held back a smile. "I studied general science," she said, "but my specialty is mineralogy." It made sense to Nancy. Mars was filled with rocks, and a mineralogist could glean some insight to the planet's past.

Except for the two commanders, the last member of the crew entered as they all sat down in their predetermined seats. Nancy thought from his posture that he had served time in the military. With a bold stride and perfect posture, he stopped at attention and proudly proclaimed, "Good morning. I am Lieutenant Zachary Knight of the United States Marine Corps." The only thing he presented himself with that was not like a Marine was his voice, toned down for the non-military presence in the small room. Once the introductions were once again made, he explained, "My specialty is weaponry. What I've been told is that we have no possible way of knowing what we may encounter, so I've been assigned for safety measures."

The six of them continued talking for several minutes before Captain Newman entered ahead of Commander Gary Singh and three men with NASA logos on their formal apparel, all of them holding clipboards and carrying pencils on their ears. Nancy had heard the rumors that Captain Newman was a tough guy, not willing to tolerate any form of disobedience and listening to few questions. He had been on three Shuttle missions, but had been pulled from the space program after being arrested as the result of a drunken revelry in a bar, part of a long string of incidents related to alcohol. Only recently had he been allowed back in the program after a year of sobriety, but not without a struggle. She glanced at the Marine and pondered the validity of the rumors. Commander Singh had trained with Captain Newman and had been on two Shuttle missions himself, including one to deploy an interplanetary rocket. She did not know much more about him, but the way he presented himself gave the impression that he was someone that most people would like to meet.

Everybody took their seats and the mission briefing began. Everyone reintroduced themselves, starting with the two commanders who had not yet met the others. Nancy was next, then Adam, Yolanda, Joe, Walker, and Zack. It turned out that although Yolanda was the first Costa Rican to fly into space, she had moved to Mexico five years ago. She was joining the American crew in conjunction with the still emerging Mexican Space Association. It was reiterated that they did not know if a hostile alien race could be encountered, so Lieutenant Knight had been assigned as a weapons expert for the journey. Even Nancy agreed with this assignment; even though she knew it was ludicrous, the old adage held true: better safe than sorry. Besides, the rumors about Captain Newman made her a touch nervous.

Once the introductions were finished, the flight controller turned on a slide projector in the wall as the room dimmed. "Your assignment is threefold," he said as the first slide lit the screen. It showed a picture of what to Nancy appeared to be a mound of dirt shaped like a head. She glanced at Joe to see a wide-eyed expression of recognition. The controller continued, "The first is to go to Mars and land in the Cydonia region. We believe that it is possible there may be evidence of a past civilization in this area. In order to land on the rocky surface, Diablo is being equipped with inflatable tires."

"Excuse me," Nancy interrupted, "but this looks like someone tossed a mask into the dirt. Is this the right picture?" Her question was meant to be heard aloud, but was directed at only one individual.

Joe turned to her and said, "True, it looks like a face. This was taken a long time ago from orbit. Nineteen seventy-nine, to be exact."

Nancy scoffed, "So what? Telescopic photography. It just happened to hit this. It's just a trick of the light."

Joe's demeanor did not change as he replied, "That could be true, but no one can be certain. This structure is a mile across."

"A mile?" voiced Adam in awe. This even surprised Nancy, who suddenly found some of her arguments rendered useless. She wanted to argue further, but decided it would be more prudent in this setting to let the matter go. They would find out when they arrived, but she convinced herself it was a natural formation.

The paranormal investigator added, "That's not all. Those three square looking things to the south of it are believed by some to be pyramids. We'll know soon enough." He obviously said the last sentence to make sure Nancy did not interrupt proceedings, so she held back the statement she was about to make.

The speaker continued, "There's a lander on its way that will arrive about two months before you. It contains fuel to refuel Diablo for your second assignment."

"That was the last mission we led," said Captain Newman with a quick glance at Commander Singh.

The projector advanced to the next slide, a montage of worlds. "These are the Jovian moons Io, Europa, Ganymede, and Callisto. It's possible that signs of life may also be found there. You are to look for life and respond; however, you are not to land unless necessary. We have launched a fuel rocket that will settle into orbit before you arrive. It was a top secret launch during a Shuttle mission five years ago."

The projector went off and the room was lit once more. "That's only two assignments," said Commander Singh. "What's the third?"

For a moment, Nancy thought she heard one of the men in the briefing room sigh. "For now," the man leading the briefing said, "you will follow the other two assignments. When you refuel at Jupiter, you will find out what the final assignment is." He took a look at his notes. "There is one more order. Soon after you leave the Earth-Moon system, we will break radio contact. We don't need a panic breaking out if anyone figures out why you've gone there."

Joe raised his hand. "Sir," he said, "there will be suspicious people anyway. There already are, in fact. Three of my colleagues have already accused me of being part of a conspiracy. What good is it to keep that part of it secret?" Nancy knew from experience that Joe suspected the question had become routine to answer.

Sure enough, he did not even look at his notes before answering, "If we were to let rumors run rampant," he answered, "we could face an epidemic of violence. By containing the available information, we can restrict the scope of the rumors. Those people who think we don't, or can't, keep any secrets will do the rest for us. Now, are there any other questions?"

"Yes," said Nancy. "I made it clear when I signed up for this mission that my lifelong intent has been to prove there are no such thing as aliens. Isn't this contradictory to that?"

The man glanced at his papers before answering, "Not really. You were chosen for that very reason. It was possible that we could select someone with an agenda, and your secondary assignment is to discover any such agendas and take the side of the nonbeliever to negate invalid arguments. You should keep somewhat of an open mind, however."

As a sensation of disgust and horror washed over her, she turned quickly to Joe. Joe glanced at her with a look that somehow combined pity, anger, frustration, sorrow, and helplessness. He angrily turned to the man briefing them and loudly murmured, "You want her to debunk me."

A silent moment passed before the speaker turned away and said, "Anything else?"

"Yeah, you can kiss my—"

"Joe!" Nancy interrupted. He had always had that attitude, and she was well-practiced to be ready for it. "We'll settle this on the mission." If he had not turned his head back to the controller, she might not have been so calm.

Commander Singh raised a finger and commented, "There's one thing that I've been wondering about. How are we going to take two years of food with us?"

"And what about oxygen?" added Walker. "Surely, the ship can't hold that many tanks. It would be too heavy, especially with that much food onboard."

The speaker simply said, "We have a new waste recycling system. Bacteria is cycled out and the waste is recycled into food. It's palatable, but it's still new technology." Everyone balked at that answer. "You'll also be carrying a number of plants on board to provide oxygen. These will be kept in the space lab until you leave orbit and will be stored there before you land on Mars. Plant food will also be produced by the recycling system. Are there any other questions?"

There was silence for a moment as Joe held his forehead. Nancy also began to feel the onset of a headache. "Very well, then," the controller continued. "The National Aeronautics and Space Administration thanks you for your service and wishes you good luck and godspeed."

As everyone else quietly rose and left, Joe slowly walked over to Nancy, still sitting and visibly shaken despite her best efforts at self control. "Are you all right?" he asked.

Nancy came out of her daze and said, "I'm fine. I just...I just thought that I was chosen for my untapped potential and what I could do." She reclined herself into the back of the chair, fighting back one of the loudest screams she could have ever produced. "Now I see I'm just a viewpoint. It hurts."

He put his arm on her shoulder as he said, "Hey, it's not that bad. There were probably a lot of people they could have chosen for that. You're the only astrophysicist we've got, so they had to choose someone who knows your field as well as you do. Doctor Flores isn't a specialist in space sciences. You are." He leaned over to her with serious eyes and added, "Besides, you'll keep me in line." He did not need to say that he would do the same to her. Perhaps they would be a good combination on this mission. "Come on, we don't launch for another six months and we don't start training until Wednesday. There's going to be a dinner at Captain Newman's house before we get down to business, so let's just have fun until then."

Chapter Two

After six months of intense training, the eight soon-to-be astronauts were very well prepared to begin their journey, but nerves still shook inside them at the thought of being so far away for so long. Nancy thought back on the good times and bad times, from Captain Newman and Commander Singh's words of encouragement to Joe's less than enthusiastic attempt at whirling around at more than twice the force of gravity; he did not even like dips in the road, much less devices that spun so fast you could barely move. His reaction afterward was both hysterical and worrisome, stumbling dizzily toward what he hoped was the bathroom with his hand covering his mouth; they had been warned to skip breakfast, but he had drunk apple juice anyway. Fortunately, two people had been on hand to carry him to his destination. A second attempt in the device proved much more successful.

Adam whined every day about how little time they allowed him to study the schematics before being thrust into hands-on study. Every time Nancy conversed with him, he had a new complaint about why he thought the design would fail. His main concern was the small size of the fuel tanks. If it was not that which he was complaining about, it was the fuel itself. If it was not the fuel, it was the stability of the pipe design. If it was not the pipe design, he found something else that he thought would be trouble. A new, stronger, lightweight material was being used for the inner mechanics, worrying him as well; much of the inside had been refitted, but the outside was still the same, heavier design.

Joe and Doctor McCrone—Walker, as he insisted on being called, though Captain Newman and Lieutenant Knight refused—had worked together, deciding upon how to use the space lab for their purposes. Nancy and Yolanda used it separately from them, so Nancy only knew what Joe told her when they had the chance to talk. Apparently, they were considering using the rear pallet as a medical bay and waited a month before approval finally came. That meant the longer, more weighty long module space lab would be used, but they later found out a new one had been designed and partly built. They persuaded NASA to finish and use it instead, with a few minor modifications for the long journey.

In Nancy's opinion, the biggest surprise was not Yolanda's eagerness, but her playfulness. She clearly took her job seriously, but at the same time had a happy-go-lucky attitude that Captain Newman found appalling. It was a wonder he had not tried to get her thrown off the mission, especially after the media incident in which she called him a drunkard. From then onward, it was always tense whenever the two of them were together. Joe was able to mediate a truce, convincing Yolanda to be more professional while Captain Newman promised to forget the event ever happened.

Now, after half a year, Nancy stood between Yolanda and Lieutenant Knight as the entire crew stared out the window toward the one hundred thirty foot structure attached to the enormous fuel tank, the two solid rocket boosters secured firmly on its side in the distance. At that moment, it was the most glorious site she had ever seen. Behind her she heard Gary ask Joe, "Sure doesn't look like it has a new engine, does it?" Without looking, she knew her friend was shaking his head in agreement. She also agreed in silence. Glances at Yolanda and Zack showed that they were both too transfixed by the visage before them to have heard the comment. She was surprised she, herself, had heard it. After a moment, she inquired, "Adam, How old is the design?"

She looked back at Adam the gloomy engineer. He was looking forward in awe, though not as much as the others. After a brief pause, he responded, "A year and a half." His eyes showed worry that she did not think possible.

"It was tested on the last Shuttle mission," said Commander Singh. "I talked with the flight commander after they got back and he said it ran fine."

Adam solemnly answered, "But that was a standard mission. They didn't even try to leave orbit."

As Captain Newman was about to respond, a man arrived from the direction of the exit from the building and said, "They're ready." He motioned through the door leading to the outside.

With a satisfied flourish of his hand, which Nancy knew from experience was from his victory in being able to be on this mission after his two-year suspension, Captain Newman motioned for them to follow. "We're ready, too," he said. It was the truth, except for Adam, who managed to hold his head up and put on a suggestion of happiness. Somehow, she thought something was behind it that he was only suppressing. She wondered why he had been selected for the mission.

They took what Nancy felt to be the longest walk of her life down the hallway to where the spectators were waiting. Once out the door, she looked at all the people who had come to wish them the best. Although it was dominated by the people they had trained under and would guide them, most of whom they would never meet, there were some former astronauts and family. A few feet down, she spotted her mother at the front of the group in tears, Joe's parents and two sisters next to her. Just as she was about to point them out to her life-long friend, he put a hand on her shoulder and pointed first. She had to fight back tears at the touch of her friend's hand. Friends had been allowed this close, a notably rare event. For a two year mission, she should not have been surprised. The tears suddenly burst as they suddenly held up a sign proclaiming their love for her and Joe. Commander Singh looked back at them with a smile.

The last group before boarding the elevator platform was the most surprising. To their right were people cheering, mostly for Joe. Wackos, obviously. But the other side was even more worrisome: Protesters, those who believed that Joe had sold them out. She ignored them both. To her surprise, Joe also ignored them. Without looking at her, he said, "I should have expected this. As soon as they told me they'd be letting people this close I should have known."

"Well," said Walker, "you have two years to figure out how to deal with them."

It shocked Nancy when Joe responded, "They're wackos. They've made up their mind, and they'll read whatever I do or don't do into whatever misbegotten ideas they've concocted. They're the ones who give people like me a bad name." Nancy wished she could see her own face as she looked at him in surprise, then regained her composure as she realized anyone could see it.

They reached the jeeps, where to their surprise the President was waiting amid the sea of reporters, photographers, paparazzi, and other media types scavenging the story of the decade. They had been told he would be there, but the first-time astronauts where still in awe. As each of them stepped up to him, he shook their hands with a simple, personalized "Good luck," except for a few words to Captain Newman she could not hear. Each of them gave their thanks, especially Adam.

After they turned and waved to everybody standing against the long walk from the building, they boarded the jeeps for their final destination. The Diablo became even more astounding as they moved closer and much smaller than they had expected. The jeeps stopped at the foot of the tower and they finally departed the small vehicles to make the glorious step onto the platform that would take them to the entrance to the craft. With a final wave to the cameras in the distance, the door closed to prevent anyone from falling off the platform.

"Here we go," Nancy joyfully murmured under her breath as they began crawling upward toward the top of the ship. She involuntarily looked at the orbiter to watch for a few seconds before leaning over to Joe and hugging him. She could tell from his reaction he was just as excited, but she was not sure if it was because he was on the mission or if he was happy that she had finally achieved her life-long dream.

With the crowd out of their sight, they began milling about the platform in apprehensive ecstasy. A few moments of silence passed before Captain Newman began speaking. "Before we enter the ship," he said, "I'd just like to say that being on this mission means a lot to me. I know that each of you was chosen from among hundreds of applicants, and that nobody would have been chosen who didn't belong." He looked over them with a sense of pride. Pride? Nancy wasn't sure. "I couldn't have chosen my own crew if I tried. During training, I kept an eye on each of you. You've all come a long way, and you all have what it takes to be on this mission." He directed the statement more toward Adam. "We'll be on our own for well over a year. After a month, we'll be cutting off contact because of how long it will take for the messages to go back and forth. By the time we get back, we'll probably all be sick of each other." He turned away and looked up, holding out his hands to the ship before them. "This will be our home for the next fifteen months. We won't be able to leave it except on Mars or to make external repairs, unless you want to be the first person lost to the vacuum of space. And I know none of you want that." He turned back. "I'm proud to have you as a crew."

The hatch was looming almost at eye level with them as he finished. "Isn't this incredible?" someone asked. It took a moment for Nancy to realize it had been Commander Singh.

After what seemed like forever, the platform came to a stop and the two members of the ground crew joined them. One turned a lever on the side of the platform and it began moving outward toward the craft. Half a minute later, the platform stopped and was manually inched forward to touch the side of the orbiter. The hatch was open, invitingly waiting for them to pass ever closer to their destiny. Commander Singh led the way so he could step over Captain Newman's chair to his seat. Captain Newman, himself, followed, then Adam—who had been named Mission Specialist—and then Nancy. She walked along the floor beside the ladder—the wall, she had to remind herself—to the flight deck and took her seat beside Adam, where she could look out between the two commanders. In the mid deck, where they entered, Yolanda and Joe would be sitting in front of Walker, and Lieutenant Knight would be in a special compartment because of the lack of seating room. "I don't think ten years of training could have prepared me for this moment," she said as she lay down in her seat.

Captain Newman looked back at her as he said, "You never get used to it. It's different every time." He then began discussing the course with Commander Singh.

She turned to Adam, who was visibly nervous. "Adam," she said, "the engines have been tested in flight. You have nothing to worry about."

Adam turned his head to her with a look of death. "I still believe what I said," he whispered. She wished she could switch places with Joe so she could talk with Yolanda and he talk with Adam.

A few minutes later, the two men in front stopped talking and simply began to wait. She had not been listening, anyway; she had just caught a word or two about it being the first flight in years for either of them and that they had both been at the initial launch of the Diablo to test the engines, the only time Captain Newman had been allowed anywhere near during his suspension. She noticed the cloudless sky through the window and realized that this was it. The weather would not interrupt the launch.

Occasional laughter could be heard from the mid deck. Of course, the attitude would not be as serious with them since they had no part in the actual launch. A short time passed before the two of them reached into the flight-data file to get the cue cards and began attaching their Velcro backs to the instrument panel. About five minutes later, the flight controller could be heard over the radio saying, "Diablo, this is launch control. Radio check. Over."

"Roger," said Captain Newman. "Out." He reached up and adjusted the channel to check his intercom, and the same routine was heard. Commander Singh did the same on his side, and had to raise the volume slightly. One last check was made, on what channel Nancy did not know or care, and silence resumed in the ship except for the occasional laughter from the mid deck that Captain Newman did not seem to approve of. Five minutes later, two more checks were made with Mission Control.

Nancy waited in silence for several more minutes after that. The laughter abated during that time, and she thought she could hear serious conversation. It sounded as if the four of them were comparing notes in preparation for Mars, which was still three months ahead.

A light came on in front of Captain Newman, startling Nancy. Something was wrong, and the flight would be delayed. Sure enough, a voice came over the intercom. It said, "Diablo, this is Launch Control. Ready abort advisory check."

Captain Newman simply laid there and said, "Roger. Check is satisfactory. Out."

Nancy gave a sigh of relief as she realized that it was not an actual abort, but a test of the indicator. She tried to listen to what was being said below. After a couple minutes, she realized that they were talking with the ground crew. Shortly after, she heard them cheer as the ground crew stepped outside and the hatch could be heard as it was sealed shut. A few seconds later, the radio squawked again. "Diablo, this is Control. Side hatch is secure."

"Roger, we copy," said Captain Newman in a voice that showed both tiredness and excitement.

Several minutes went by, the mid deck now quiet with anticipation. Another five minutes passed before she saw Captain Newman reach to something where she could not see. Almost immediately, a gauge began moving as the air began to feel thicker. Once it stopped, he said, "Control, this is Diablo. We show cabin pressure nominal. Over."

"Roger. Out," said the flight controller. With the check for leaks in the cabin, she now knew there was just over an hour remaining. Normally, the internal measurement check would be next, but that would be skipped since this was an interplanetary mission. Nancy noticed it was wrong, however, and suggested, "Do you think we should do a measurement check, anyway?"

The pair of front both took a look at the instrument and looked at each other. When the appointed time arrived, T minus 51 minutes, they checked anyway. Launch Control was flabbergasted that they were worried about it, and all the blame was put on Nancy. Finally, they suggested that they make the proper adjustment just in case it was needed "for some weird reason." Nancy thought it was curious since they would probably need it upon their return. She wished she could get Joe's opinion. A moment later, she came to her senses and mentally scolded herself.

Immediately afterward came the next phase of the launch sequence as Commander Singh reached to his side and she heard a group of switches flip. "Boiler control switch on." Another group of switches was heard. "Nitrogen supply switch on." A third group of switches. Strange, Joe had told her there were only two. "Propheletyline switch on. Over."

"Roger. Out."

The two men looked at each other, then back at the other two on the flight deck. "Now we wait," Captain Newman said. Nancy just gave a nod.

She looked at Adam to see his eyes showing hints of terror; he was apparently afraid something would go wrong with the new fuel system. Then again, he was afraid of many things, not the least of which was them not coming back. "What's wrong?" she whispered to him.

Adam leaned over to her so the others would not hear. "I'm not so sure about this 'propheletyline' they've got. I don't think it's stable. I know I'm not exactly the most encouraging person to have on the mission, but this is one thing I'm fairly sure about." A chill coursed through her veins as he straightened in her seat. She was elated the orbiter wasn't equipped with a rear view mirror where they could see the panic on her face. She wasn't sure if it was because it was because of the person she was talking to or the possibility that he had actually stumbled onto something that could prove to be fatal.

Nearly twenty minutes passed before time for action came again. A light came on above Captain Newman's head. He said, "Control," he said, "this is Diablo. Computer activation complete. Flight backup complete. Over."

Once more, the Controller said, "Roger. Out." Captain Newman then reached down to the pad directly in front of her and flipped a switch to the down position, then punched four keys on the keyboard next to him.

Nancy thought about what would be going on back on the ground. She looked at the clock to see that there were about thirty-two minutes left. By now, the ground crew and all visitors were being cleared for launch. A smatter of laughter came from the mid deck, breaking the tension of the coming lift-off which Adam's nervous twitching amplified in turn. She only planned to take his hand for a moment, but the almost painful grip he gave it told her he needed much longer.

She wondered what they were talking about everywhere. Doubtless, those on the crew deck were discussing what they would do once in space or once they returned, or they were talking about each other. Control was undeniably all business, while those who had come just to see the launch were probably talking about all sorts of things. An unusually high number of former astronauts had come to see the launch, and they were probably discussing former missions and the details of this one. Cost and efficiency were the most commonly discussed issues, but at that point cost was no longer an issue unless the launch was aborted. Once they were out of contact, efficiency was their own problem.

"Diablo, this is Control. Ground crew is secure. Over."

Commander Singh acknowledged it as Captain Newman pressed two buttons beside him, then reached for something to his left. An alarm sounded. Adam would have jumped out of the ship if Nancy had not been holding his hand. "Control," said Captain Newman as he watched a gauge fall, "this is Diablo. OMS pressure on." He waited a few moments. "Cabin vent complete. Over."

"Roger. We see it. Out."

Adam's sigh startled even the commanders. Captain Newman smiled as he looked back, saying, "Nervous, are we?"

Adam looked forward and simply nodded. The two men smiled as they gave each other an amused look.

A minute later, three short screams came from the mid deck. Nancy unstrapped and began moving to the access as Captain Newman began speaking in chopped tones, "Control, this is Diablo. Something has happened on the mid deck. We are checking it out."

Nancy barely heard the acknowledgment as she passed through the egress to see several pieces of foam rubber had fallen and Walker had his stethoscope in his hand. She looked up to see Joe and Yolanda each holding something of the physician's and a locker door hanging down above Yolanda. "How did this happen?" she asked.

Yolanda was moving to stand in her chair to reach the locker. "It came open suddenly," she said. "It must have been closed wrong."

"We'd better check all of them," Nancy said. "We can't afford having anything breaking free, especially during lift-off." Joe and Walker were both already standing on their chairs. Nancy handed the foam rubber to Walker and moved back to the passage. "Captain," she said, "a locker came open and everything fell out. Joe and—Mister Rommel and Doctor Flores are checking all of them."

Once Captain Newman passed word along, Control asked, "Was there any damage?"

Nancy stood on her seat said into Captain Newman's microphone, "Negative. Fortunately, everything fell on Doctor Flores and what she couldn't grab was caught before it hit the bottom."

"Make sure and report," Control responded. "We are continuing countdown."

Nancy went back into the mid deck, where Lieutenant Knight had emerged from the vertical bunk—it had been redesigned to double as a launch seat because there were only three seats available for launch— and was watching in case anything else fell. Sure enough, three other compartments had not been completely closed. Walker and Yolanda acted professionally, but Joe cursed a blue streak. Lieutenant Knight nodded in agreement with his opinion, but the firm look on his face said that Joe's language was well beyond the limits.

Once those on the mid deck resecured themselves, Nancy went back onto the flight deck and told everyone what happened. The countdown continued unabated, and the conversation was considered the Captain's voice check. Commander Singh performed his voice check and silence again dominated the ship, this time permeated by a humming from Captain Newman, the tune of a song that had been a hit many years ago. If she remembered correctly, it dealt with a man who could fly, feeling free as a bird as someone else saw and watched in disbelief. She decided it was appropriate. A moment later, Commander Singh joined in verbally. Captain Newman started singing, then Adam to her surprise. Although not much for music, Nancy joined them. As they got louder, they began hearing everyone on the mid deck join them. Near the end of the song, Captain Newman flipped another switch. As they were ending, even Adam was in high spirits. Well, for him, anyway.

This time the silence was total and lasted for several minutes. They were in the ten minute hold, when the countdown was stopped at T minus twenty minutes to catch up on anything on which they had fallen behind. At the end, Control said, "Diablo, we are resuming countdown."

"Roger," said Captain Newman.

Commander Singh flipped a switch on the center panel, then hit some buttons on the keyboard. A flight trajectory appeared on the screen above his head. "Control, this is Diablo. Flight plan is loaded into the computer." After the acknowledgment, he hit the same keyboard pattern a second time. Captain Newman hit a switch over his head, then hit more buttons on the keyboard. The pilot said, "Flight trajectory. Check."

An icy chill went through Nancy's body as the realization of what was about to happen finally hit her. She completely relaxed her body and thought back on all the years since she and Joe had first met and argued over the existence of everything from aliens to telekinesis to astral projection. She had never believed anything of the sort possible and vowed on that day she would prove him wrong. She decided she would find it in all her years of astronomical study if there was anything to his beliefs, and she had never seen anything. One of her colleagues had died in a suspicious car crash after claiming he had seen something one night they watched the sky together, even though he never said what it was. She had analyzed his data, and it was confusing. It was probably just a secret government project, but those were best left untouched; after all, it was national defense. She told the media she had not seen it, but some did not believe her. When she had mentioned it to Joe during training, he froze for a moment before saying that her belief was a possibility. She barely noticed Captain Newman flipping more switches during her time of thought. Finally, an involuntarily large smile bridged her ears before she saw Adam staring at her in wonder. Emotions ripped her body in half as she took a deep breath and regained her composure, even though part of the smile refused to leave.

"Diablo, this is Control. We will control the abort check. Over." The abort light came on and dimmed, then turned off. The cycle occurred two more times.

"Roger, looks good," said Captain Newman.

Two or three laughs broke the ensuing silence for the next few minutes before Commander Singh sighed. "Don't worry," he said as he looked back, "this is the dullest part of the mission."

Almost resignedly, Adam replied, "I hope so. How long has it been since we boarded?"

Nancy knew, but she left the answer to the two experienced astronauts. "About two hours," said Captain Newman. "We've just started the second of two ten minute holds so everyone can get caught up on anything they may have fallen behind on. We're at T minus nine minutes and holding."

Adam's questioning, worried expression was no surprise to Nancy from what she had just heard. He asked, "Why couldn't they keep up? Why do we have to give them time?"

Neither astronaut seemed surprised; both of them had come to know him well over the past six months. Nancy would have given anything to know what was on their minds. Captain Newman answered, "Sometimes something comes up on the ground that has nothing to do with us. That can take a minute or two away and make them fall behind. Sometimes they have to clear someone who wandered into the launch area. That's usually all it is." She noticed he did not mention the possibility of doing one last check from Control or technical problems on the ground. Adam was about to inquire further, but she squeezed his hand before he could.

With difficulty, she listened to the chit chat from below, an almost inaudible, muffled voice apparently belonging to Lieutenant Knight. They were talking about the possibilities of what they might find on this mission. Most of the conversation belonged to Joe and Yolanda, but occasionally Walker or Lieutenant Knight would make a comment that prevented an argument from starting. The main thing they agreed upon, however, was that whatever was discovered would be exciting, and they would be the ones to make those discoveries.

Nancy looked at the clock to see that only a few seconds remained in the hold. As she dug her head into the headrest, Adam quietly muttered, "I'm not worried about the launch." She could tell she was not meant to hear. "I don't think I had enough time looking at the engine. I hardly saw the schematics."

Nancy turned her head to him, much to his surprise, and said, "It's just another small advance in technology that's been blown out of proportion. The last assignment is probably just to test it coming back from Jupiter. Remember, you're mission specialist." They put their helmets on, the last to do so, and braced for launch, as Nancy pondered why they had not chosen Joe as the specialist.

Just then, Captain Newman reached down to flip a switch and a timer in front of her began counting down. "Control, this is Diablo. Event timer stared. Over."

This was it. She felt excitement and tension shock its way through the ship. Adam was hurting her hand. She tapped him and he let go. She shook her hand as he apologized. It would be soon, now. Very soon.

All Nancy's concentration was on the countdown before her. Eight thirty-one. Eight thirty. Eight twenty-nine. The involuntary smile spread across her face again as Adam muttered a silent prayer to whatever gods there may be. Everyone on the mid deck was silent. Eight twenty. She closed her eyes for a few seconds in elated bliss. When she opened them again it read eight minutes and thirteen seconds.

She waited a few more seconds before Commander Singh reached to his side where she could not see and she thought she heard three switches through her helmet. T minus eight minutes. Another minute and the access arm would retract. Her nerves began to fray, and her self control tried to falter. She closed her eyes for a long time, listening to the conversation about the prestart of the auxiliary power units, or APUs, then several more switches. She had never heard so many switches being used in her life. In a way, she hoped she would again, though she suspected that thought might change during the mission.

She opened her eyes just as the procedure to power the APUs began, no longer listening to the conversation. She was too excited. She glanced at Adam to see that his eyes were squeezed shut in what looked like aggravation.

It caught her attention when Control informed them they were now on internal power. She relegated herself to staring at the timer and listening to the conversations with Ground Control. A few seconds later, the hydraulic equipment was confirmed to be out of the way.

At last, Control said, "Diablo, main engine gimbal complete." Adam grimaced in fear beside her; the engines had swiveled to their launch positions. A few moments later, Ground Control confirmed in technical jargon that the oxygen tanks were closed.

Nearly another minute passed before the radios were reduced to a level that the two commanders liked and Commander Singh flipped yet another switch. She knew from her talks with Joe that it was the switch that prevented automatic shutdowns. Abort was now impossible. It possessed a strange excitement to her. An incredible thrill went through her entire person as she heard, "Diablo, this is Control. H-two tank pressurization OK. You're go for launch. Over."

She continued to listen as she watched the counter, the excitement continuing to build within her. It was all she wanted to do. No other thoughts crossed her mind. When the countdown reached twenty-five seconds, she did not need the confirmation from Control to know that the computers now had full control. Again, silence fell within the flight deck, but she knew how short lived it would be. At six seconds, the Controller began counting down to launch. Two point two seconds later, a roar caused the ship to vibrate. T minus two. One. Zero. T plus one. Two. A stronger vibration coursed through the ship. Everything outside seemed to retract down into the ground. Smoke billowed past the windows. The spire on top of the tower began to slide down past the window. Her entire body was pressed solidly into her seat. Mere seconds later, Control reported they had cleared the tower and they were looking good. They rolled into the upside down position, which she would not have realized if she could not see the ground above them through the edge of the window; the pressure from the thrust was creating an artificial gravity that held them in place. It was hard to believe only half a minute had passed.

Even less time was added into the flight when she felt the pressure lighten, indicating the engines had reduced their output. She just heard Captain Newman give a verbal confirmation over the rumble. Only a few seconds later, they would reach "max Q," whatever that meant, and the engines would roar back to full power. Sure enough, the pressure shortly resumed.

As the sky slowly darkened from its baby blue to a purplish haze, she felt the thrust lessen then pick back up again as the solid rocket boosters were released. The coursing rumble seared through her body, capturing her concentration. She hardly realized how much time had passed when Captain Newman reported that they could reach orbit with only one main engine—T plus seven minutes, if she remembered correctly.

Just as she thought she would be crushed under the pressure, the engines reduced power. Good thing, too, as she had no doubt her life was about to flash before her eyes. About a minute and a half later, three red lights came on and the rumbling stopped. She wanted to listen further to make sure that it was the scheduled event instead of a malfunction, and Adam's nervousness made it even worse. Their fears died when Captain Newman said, "Roger. Main engine cut-off on schedule. Out."

Only seconds later, a clank vibrated the ship and she saw the tip of the external tank vanish as it was released. She relaxed. So did Adam, who took her hand again to soothe his always fluttering nerves. A few more minutes of changing computer programs and maneuvering, and they were in their preliminary orbit.

Chapter Three

"Okay, let's start setting up everything," said Captain Newman. "We're only supposed to be in orbit for six hours before leaving orbit, and I don't want to fall behind on anything we're supposed to do."

Nancy was the first to remove her seat restraint and float down to the mid deck. Yolanda was already floating around, but Joe and Zack were both complaining to her about the possibility of the ship not being in its proper orbit yet. Walker agreed with a simple frown. Upon Nancy's appearance on the mid deck, Yolanda stuck out her tongue at the others. "Having fun?" Nancy asked.

The scientist twirled in several directions and said, "Yes! I've never felt so free in my life!"

As she began to move toward at the lockers, Nancy said, "Then let's start unpacking. We have to get ready to leave orbit in six hours, and I don't think any of us want Captain Newman on our backs." As they all unfastened themselves and floated to the lockers, she asked, "How long had you been out of your seat, Yolanda?"

"Not long," was the answer. "I heard Captain Newman talking and thought we were in orbit."

As each of them began pulling out whatever they were supposed to set up, Adam and Gary entered and began to retrieve the suits for space walking. "Joe," said Gary, "how much do you know about motion photography?"

Joe's smile told them all they needed to know. "My specialty is crop circles," he said. "Part of investigating them is setting up cameras to record them being formed. I've learned so much I could probably work in Hollywood."

"Get your suit on," Gary said. "We're supposed to set up a series of cameras on the outside of the ship."

Closing the locker, Joe responded, "I figured I'd be in on it. After all, moving and securing plants doesn't take six hours." As they left, she heard Gary asking how well Joe understood the solar panels.

Nancy was surprised that Gary gave a brief laugh as they began putting on their suits, then remained quiet. Silence continued until they had left for the mid deck to leave the ship. She then broke the silence when she saw Yolanda fiddling with some knobs in the waste management compartment, which Nancy hoped they would just call the bathroom. "What are you doing?" she asked.

Yolanda answered, "I have to check the recycling system to see that it is working properly." She closed the door, herself inside.

Nancy puckered her lips and quickly turned to Walker and Zack. To her surprise, the Marine was checking to make sure his enormous stash of weaponry was intact. He glared at each of his firearms fervently, picking up each one in turn to make sure no damage had occurred to it during the launch. He then replaced it and moved on to the next one.

Walker held some of his equipment in a tight bag. "Would you mind helping me take these to the medical area?" he asked Nancy.

"Sure," she said as she took a bag filled with packages of gauze and cotton, surprised at how light it felt in the weightlessness. Only its natural inertia gave her any sense that it was even there. She followed him to the mid deck, where Joe was just closing the hatch to the airlock. They could not hear the air being evacuated, but a clang let them know that the trio was beginning their mission. She followed the doctor back to the aft end of the mid deck, where a large desk was set into the back wall. He let the bag float, then opened the drawers and began filling them with various items from the bag. It was not even half of the equipment he had brought. She would not have been surprised if he had brought lollipops.

As Walker took the jars from Nancy, he said, "I'll get the rest. You do whatever you're supposed to. Thank you."

"You're welcome," Nancy said as she swam back to the space lab to look through the storage compartments. About five hundred of them sat above the table seats and along the wall, the crew using some of them to store personal items they had brought on their journey. She looked in hers first; she had only taken a few items, and only five drawers were needed. The highest one contained enough feminine hygiene to last her the entire journey and more; she was sure that Yolanda had done the same and that Joe would try to figure out the combination to both of their lockers. Through the rest of her drawers, there was nothing that was more important to her than that vital part of female life.

A sound behind her made her slam the door much harder than Gary would approve of; indeed, there seemed to be a momentary jerk in the ship's orbit. She spun around to see that she had scared Yolanda half to death. Both of them closed their eyes in relief and sighed. "I'm sorry," they both said at once.

Nancy opened her eyes to see a leather Bible was floating next to Yolanda. "The system seems to be working," Yolanda said, "so I decided to do some reading on the mid deck while waiting to see what developed." She retrieved the Christian holy book as she said, "I hope to read this all the way through several times before we get back."

At about that time, Walker came flying past them on his way back from the mid deck, hauling two more bags. "This is all there is," he said. "I'll be spending the next few hours setting up the medical area."

As he moved back into his office, Yolanda said, "I'll be on the mid deck if I'm needed." She left quietly.

Nancy began looking through the general use compartments. Several contained enough cleaning products for an army. These were dry cleaning products for both themselves and their suits. Another contained dry rags, another held towels, and several more contained toilet paper made especially for the recycling system. The thought of it sickened her again, but she knew she had to adjust to it. Others contained entertainment, much of it magnetic. Dominoes, cards, chess, backgammon, and some tile game she had never seen before. Two pairs of headphones that plugged into the workstation accentuated the hundreds of compact disks in one drawer. Movies on digital video discs were crammed into another. Plenty of paper, pens, pencils, and sharpeners were in another drawer. Still another drawer contained all sorts of tools.

After about an hour, the airlock hatch opened to allow the three space walkers back into the ship. "It's done," Joe said. "We can see in any direction at will from the flight deck, now. We won't have to worry about turning the onboard cameras if something bad comes our way. The only problem is that we'll have to do all this again before landing on Mars and after taking off again."

Finishing her review, Nancy said, "That's good to hear. Not that we'll need that much warning in the vacuum of space."

"True," said Joe, "but you never know." She knew exactly what he was referring to, and she wanted to vomit.

Just then, Gary leaned back to them and said, "Joe, you stay here and begin moving some plants to the mid deck. Everyone else, Captain Newman wants you on the flight deck."

Only one hour had passed as they all went forward and up into the flight deck. Captain Newman was floating dominantly at the front of the deck. Once everyone had arrived, he said, "It's now eleven in the morning. We leave in four hours. Gary, you're done, are you not?"

"Yes, sir," the pilot said.

Captain Newman told him, "Then go ahead and get some sleep. Doctor Licht, you too if you're done. Since you sleep while the rest of us are awake, I'd like to go ahead and start getting on that schedule. Doctor Flores, have you checked the recycling system?"

Yolanda held up what looked like a chocolate bar and said, "It's working fine, as far as I can tell." Nancy turned away as she took a bite. "Could use salt, though."

Captain Newman nodded and said, "As long as it works. Mister Rommel, how do the plants look?"

Joe hovered halfway through the interdeck access with a radish plant in one hand and a mustard in the other. He said, "Most of them look fine. I think a couple of the carrot plants were crushed during the launch." He fastened the mustard to a series of bracing hooks in the ceiling, equipped with tiny magnets to pull at the iron in the roots to make them grow in a "downward" direction.

The captain looked at Nancy and said, "Doctor Villareal, how are the stocked goods?"

"Everything checks out," Nancy said.

"Mister McCrone," Captain Newman continued, "do the new engines check out?"

Adam said, "I didn't see any visible damage outside."

With a nod, the flight commander said, "Good. In that case, we will be leaving on schedule."

Chapter Four

It had taken Nancy four days of starving except for the occasional rationed vegetable, but she had finally forced herself to eat the food recycled from…she decided it was better not to think about it. It bore a strong similarity to chocolate, but lacked the sweetness that made the confection so addictive. Nor was it either smooth or hard, but somehow managed to fall somewhere inbetween. No illness had resulted from it, unless it caused Joe's sickness a month into the journey—two months ago—which Walker had been unable to diagnose. Everyone had hoped it was not the food; none of them dared mention the possibility of a virus until her friend had recovered.

She quietly took the stick of stiff slop from Joe as she climbed out of the bottom, upside-down bunk. They stayed quiet so as not to awaken Captain Newman, who still had another two hours to rest. She had grown accustomed to having to pull herself out of the sleep restraint and sleep station in zero gravity. Although she was required to wear a sleep suit, she found it bulky and pulled it off after she closed the screen. Once she realized the others would all be busy, she decided to exit the compartment before retrieving her suit. Joe always averted his eyes, but she often caught him taking a peek. It had been meant to be only once, but once weightlessness had begun to satisfy her opinion of herself, she decided to spend more time *au natural.*

That morning, day eighty-seven, felt different. The day before, they realized that they could now identify the planet they were destined for by simple sight. The vision of it must be prominent by now, their seven mile per second flight bringing it ever closer.

As always, she used her full forty-five minutes in preparing herself for the day ahead, which consisted almost entirely of monitoring the specialist station. Occasionally, she noticed their target point was slightly off center and a slight course correction would be made. It was the only excitement the pilot's seat ever saw. She broke the monotony by playing cards while watching the external cameras whenever Gary was in charge.

Everyone had changed to a first name basis and had come to know each other well. Yolanda and Zack had formed a bond, Joe and Walker continued to develop possible scenarios for Mars, and Adam had taken several space walks as part of his consistent study of the engine. He also remained wary of the food recycling system.

Since their sleep periods were at the same time, Joe and Nancy always ended the day playing pinochle. She did some flirting with him. It was limited because Yolanda was rising during their forty-five minutes allotted, and when she did he brushed it aside with a sly grin that confused and absolutely frustrated her.

A number of books had been provided on the computer system, but there had been little time or opportunity to read. Joe, Zack, and Adam had been able to make more time than the others, but only Joe had been able to finish *A Tale of Two Cities*. Nancy did not know what Adam was reading, but Zack had been enthralled by *The Winds of War*. She wondered when she would finish *Doctor Zhivago*. Surely, there would be plenty of time eventually. Yolanda had become engrossed in stage dramas, her favorites being by Tennessee Williams and Henrik Ibsen. Walker sometimes had to tend to a random event, such as when a screwdriver hit Joe in the eye and cut the lid, or when Gary—who spent most of his spare time watching movies—sneezed so hard he went spinning and smashed his head against the door frame. He struck so hard that Rick had to make adjustments to stop the ship from rotating.

Rick was an entirely different story. He remained all business, his only concession being the use of his first name. If he saw someone lazing, he would find something for them to do; if there was nothing to do, he would show them some of the intricacies of the technical details of the ship. Nancy had been a frequent trainee, and was now considered third in line for the pilot's chair although Joe's understanding of what happened greatly surpassed hers.

Much of the activity took place in the space lab. Walker had to finish moving all his emergency equipment from the lockers to the rear after leaving orbit, converting it into an almost fully equipped treatment center. It was their only source of medical help. For that reason, they nicknamed it "the hospital."

So far only Walker had any good reason to use the empty storage compartments in the space lab, but he had managed to stuff almost everything into the six foot wide, twelve foot deep medical bay. They kept the cards, chess set, and other materials not related to the mission in the drawers so Rick would not find them. Gary had brought a magnetic Mah Jongg set—the tile game Nancy had been wondering about—which he, Joe, Yolanda, and Walker had taken up playing often whenever Rick was piloting. The addictive game had threatened to cut into their work time, but Zack's entrance after his rest period was always the sign to put it away.

Joe, to his amusement, had become Walker's nurse. Joe had some male chauvinism in him, but Nancy found some of it appealing for some strange reason that made her feel ill. He found himself grimly studying the medical database and taking instruction from Walker much of the time. Nancy found it more amusing than the others, which she felt little shame for; he had chided her about suggesting he become a nurse when they were little, calling it a "girly job" to her face. He had risen above that, but he still held on to some of the less serious fancies. She was happy he had no objections to her chosen profession; just her goal.

"Penny for your thoughts," came the quiet voice of her companion as he faced to her side. Nancy glanced up at the top bunk where Rick slept and the horizontal bunk that Yolanda had pulled closed just before she pulled herself out of her upside-down accommodations. "Don't worry. They both use earplugs. As long as we don't speak too loud, they won't hear us."

The astrophysicist realized she had been eating her food bar quickly and stopped. With the mention of the others, she suddenly felt an incredible desire to put her suit on, which she did rapidly as she said, "I was just thinking. How big is it?" Realizing her state of dress, she immediately added, "Mars, I mean?" as she moved to pat the choking xenobiologist's back. "How big does it look?"

Joe swallowed—hard—and answered, "It looked like a small ni— light bulb in the sky." He took a rather large bite of his food bar.

Nancy finished putting on her cooling-ventilation garment and let herself slowly drift past Joe's ear. "I don't mind," she whispered. He almost spat out his food.

She drifted up to the flight deck, where the other spacefarers had all gathered to look at the sight before them. She waited for Joe to join her before rising far enough to see the planet ahead. It was off center, which was to be expected given their intercept course. As Joe had said, it looked like a ten watt, reddish-orange light bulb amid the tiny specks of light surrounding them. From this distance, she could just see the markings of the planet's larger features.

"It's only two more days," said Gary as he noticed their arrival. "Just in time, too. We don't have much fuel left. Enough for landing, but not much more."

Joe had to remind her to finish her personal hygiene. She returned to the mid deck and stripped again, this time feeling even more free than Yolanda ever had.

Nancy was surprised by Rick's willingness to let people stare at the planet ahead of them, even if only for a minute or two. He had allowed her in the pilot's seat for a few minutes while he checked something in the space lab; she was barely able to alert the avid game players by sending an SOS signal through to a console beside the table.

During the time to herself, there was never any need to adjust their course, though Rick would not have been happy if she had done so. When the thought of checking the instruments did not occur to her, she studied the glowing orb ahead of them. Judging from the apparent change in position from a few hours earlier, she estimated they had about a day and a half to go. Rick would be awakened early on Tuesday and everyone would strap themselves in for the landing. Within forty-eight hours, they would be walking on the surface of this world. A terrifying thought occurred to her.

Rick returned to the flight deck with no indication that he had seen the game below, which the others must be returning to by now. "Everything check out?" she asked.

"Fine," answered the captain. "Just wanted to see how exited the others were getting. I must have really scared them during this trip. As soon as they saw me, they jumped out of their seats." Nancy had to hold back a look of relief and the urge to blab. "Yolanda nearly came unglued when I asked why one of the storage compartments was hanging open." He let out a short laugh. "I really should be more careful with my attitude."

Nancy was glad Rick was looking forward so he could not see her widened eyes as she stared at him. This was definitely not what she had expected from him, especially after the past three months. "I'll be relieving myself," she said as she left.

Joe was the only one Nancy saw on the mid deck, but the door to the waste compartment was closed. "Who's in there?" she asked.

Joe looked up from a copy of Scientific American he had brought with him and said, "Yolanda. She's always in there." He looked back at the article and muttered something about typical females she was not meant to hear.

Nancy floated over to him and asked, "What are you reading?"

With a quick glance, he answered, "An article on time. We know that an object's velocity affects time, but one of my passions is finding out why."

"Any theories?" Nancy asked, half-expecting to hear nonsense.

Joe squinted at the page and shook his head. "No," he answered. "At least, nothing substantial. Just a hunch."

"And that is…?" She knew she would regret asking.

He looked at her, the magazine in one hand, and explained, "This article proposes that there's another element to it. She thinks there's some unknown between motion and time, and she postulates that it's gravity. I should get in touch with her when we get back."

Surprisingly, Nancy agreed with him. It was a fascinating theory if there was the slightest possibility that it was true, and Nancy considered the possibility. "What do you miss most about home?" she asked.

A moment went by before Joe looked up from the periodical. A moment after that he said, "I miss Bob Barker," and returned to the article.

She was glad he did not see the look of surprise on her face, but she, too, had been a fan during her college years. "I miss pasta," she said. "Chicken ravioli in pesto with three cheeses and a side of Italian bread with a glass of red wine. That's what I miss most."

"My office," Joe said. "It's boring, here. There aren't any unknowns. Granted, it's been getting more exciting now that we're so close to Mars, but then we have another four month wait on the way to Jupiter." He sighed as he let go of the magazine. "I miss the unknown." He looked at Nancy with abandon. "I'm a problem solver. There's nothing to solve out here in the middle of nowhere. We can't make any progress until we're settled into orbit around Mars. If there was some unknown, I'm sure I could use it to find some way to improve our situation. That's what my profession is about. In your own way, so's yours. So are Yolanda's, Walker's, and Adam's. We advance through discovering and understanding the unknown, even if it's just finding out who's knocking at the front door."

Nancy stared at Joe for a moment. So, after all those years, he was not as crazy as she thought he was—he was a scientist at heart. For the first time, she thought she could understand him, maybe even work with him on this mission instead of against him. She gave him a teary-eyed hug, but she cut it short as Yolanda opened the door to the waste compartment.

Chapter Five

The red planet continued to seemingly grow at an increasing rate over the following thirty-six hours. Most of the time, anyone with little or nothing to do went to the flight deck to watch the planet grow before their eyes, now blanketing a large portion of the sky. Naturally, they had to do so during Rick's sleep period, those eight hours being both the most relaxing and stressful time on their journey so far. Whenever Rick was scheduled to rise, he wasted no time going to the flight deck.

Only an hour remained before they would begin the landing procedure. This was the most worrisome part of the journey; the plan called for the ship to land on inflatable rubber tires made especially for the rocky Martian landscape, then take off again with fuel carried inside a lander that was considered experimental when it was launched. Adam knew how to safely refuel the ship, but still worried about how unstable he thought the propheletyline was.

Everything had been stored for landing. Rick, Nancy, Yolanda, and Gary were on the flight deck; the others had begun setting up their seats for landing, Zack preparing his specially prepared bunk for landing. The planet's features were dominant, the satellite Phobos nearby. "What do you think, Nancy?" asked Rick. "How does it look to you?"

Nancy looked at the planet carefully as their orbit took them past the tiny satellite. "I don't see any dust storms," she said. "No visible weather problems." She peered out, searching. "I'm not sure where the landing area is." She called down to the mid deck, "Joe, can you help us up here?"

"Sure," the paranormal expert called from the mid deck. He drifted up through the access a few seconds later to find the two ladies in the back of the compartment.

Nancy hated herself for asking Joe, but she did anyway. "You've studied this area. How well do you know the landscape?"

"Real well," he said as he drifted to them. "I could identify the general area from here, but I won't be able to pinpoint it. I'm glad it's in the computer." He stepped up between the two captains and peered out for several seconds. "I don't see it," he finally said. "Wait, there it is to the right. Those patches of light areas."

Gary compared the map on the screen above him to the landscape below and pointed. "Yep," he said, "there it is. Calling up the landing program." He punched in a code on the keypad.

A few moments later, Joe—whom she had not seen leave the deck—returned with a pair of binoculars and began searching the area visually. Once it was out of sight a few minutes later, he lowered them and shook his head. "Didn't see anything that could tell us where the landing site is," he said, "but I can tell you it's clear as a bell down there."

Everyone seemed unfazed by this except, understandably, for Adam. Rick looked at Gary and asked, "When are we supposed to begin retrofire?"

Gary looked back at the others before saying, "You'd better get to your seats." The others quickly returned to the mid deck to prepare for landing on the barren world above. Below. Wherever. It was confusing. Once they left, Gary leaned over to Rick and said almost out of her hearing, "You know the problem with the inflatable wheels. Are you sure you want to go through with this?" Nancy stared forward, glad they could not see her face.

"I know," Rick whispered back, "but we have an assignment. We're the first ones ever to venture this far into space, and that gives us a responsibility. If we don't have proof that we landed, it could dishearten the entire country. Do you really want that, especially with how far China has gotten?"

A quick glance at Adam showed that he was completely horrified. Obviously, Gary's statement to prepare for landing had been meant simply to get the others off the flight deck so they would not worry. The inflatable tires were designed to roll over the rocky Martian surface safely and were more tear resistant than any other material used in inflatable items. At L minus thirty seconds, the wheels would inflate for a safe landing. She leaned over to Adam and quietly asked, "Do you have any idea what's wrong?"

The engineer leaned over and answered in an even quieter whisper, "When I took one of my space walks to look over the ship, I took a look at the wheel assembly. I discovered that one of the wheels had a place on it that appeared to be stretched. It could explode during the landing."

Nancy slowly sank deeper into her seat. So that was what they were talking about. More carelessness in preparation for the flight. Instead of replacing it as they should have, they used a defective tire that was too dangerous for a mission like this. Hopefully it would hold, but if it did not the rocks on the ground would be the difference in whether they ever returned or not.

Nancy barely noticed Rick call to the mid deck to make sure every-one was secure, which they were. About five minutes later, the ship began its rotation until it was flying backwards. Gary did it by turning on the yaw; Nancy instead had expected him to pitch forward or back-ward. The computer then fired the thrusters for a few seconds to reduce the ship's velocity. She momentarily felt the ship begin to descend as the ship was turned back around. Gary then pointed the ship downward, aiming at the entry point.

Nancy's thoughts strayed to the mid deck, where Joe was. Silently, she wished he was back home on Earth doing whatever he did in his cho-sen field, however erroneous it was. The last thing she wanted was a friend hurt, much less a friend she loved. *Loved.* She had never thought of that word before. To her, it was almost foreign. She had thought she had loved before, but it always turned out to be nothing more than lustful sex. With Joe, it was different. What was it? She was afraid to know, given his chosen career path.

Gary's voice broke her concentration as he warned them that they were about to enter the atmosphere. She braced herself, thinking about the inflatable wheels. Adam was sweating as if they were on their way to the sun, obviously concerned about the same thing she was. She was not proud of it, but she was glad that she would be unable to hold his hand to comfort him during the hopeful landing.

As they were approaching a few minutes later, Gary swung the ship toward their target area and continued the descent. After a minute, the area came into clear focus. There was no doubt about it; it was a face. Not only that, but there were what appeared to be a number of pyramids, some collapsed, but from that distance it was impossible to be certain. Nancy remained convinced that they were all natural formations, but she was at a loss as to how the pyramids could have been formed. The others would all want more solid evidence, but she knew that Joe would be convinced anyway.

Finally, Rick spotted the lander on a long strip of land covered with more rocks than she could begin to count. "Hold tight," he said. He seemed as if he wanted to say something else, but she heard nothing. Gary pressed a button and a snakelike hiss of air filled the ship as the wheels inflated. She thought she heard Adam gulp. The ship began to angle upward for landing.

"Touchdown in ten," said Gary. "Nine. Eight. Seven. Six. Five. Four. Th—" He was cut off as the ship bumped against the ground early, causing Nancy to suddenly feel violent instincts toward the pilot. Sheer terror overwhelmed the thoughts of senseless violence as she suddenly envisioned one of the wheels exploding during the landing, but the jarring was only momentary. Rick gradually slowed the ship, bringing it to a stop a minute later. It was too gradual for Nancy's taste, but they could not take the chance of sliding on the dirt. Nancy put her head on Adam's shoulder, while the man next to her closed his eyes in relief. A cry of victory screamed in Spanish came from the mid deck.

Rick rose out of his seat and loudly proclaimed, "Okay, first one in their environment suit gets to set foot on the planet first." The ensuing mad rush was filled with glee as they all raced to see who would have the honor of being the first person on Mars. Nancy had to fight Gary, both of them virtually diving head first toward the ladder and startling Yolanda as they slid down the ladder together. Rick was the only one not hurrying. All of them raced into their suits and were almost in them when a loud, proud voice screamed, "*¡Viva Mexico!*" They all turned to see Yolanda fully dressed and already at the crew hatch, waiting to go outside.

"Just be patient, Yolanda," Rick said, almost in his suit. "We all have to get ready before we can let you out. We don't want anyone getting atmospheric poisoning." Yolanda impatiently understood and nodded, then began screaming at the slowpokes in the room.

Gary finished next and said, "So what do you think we're going to find out there?"

"Rocks," Nancy seriously replied.

Walker walked to the door beside Yolanda and said, "Hopefully, we won't encounter any alien germs. That's the greatest danger. Commander, I'd like to take air and soil samples and look for bacteria."

Joe told Walker, "You'll have to look underneath the rocks for bacteria. There's no ozone layer on Mars, so nothing can even exist in the sunlight." At Adam's inquiry, Joe explained that the ozone blocked ultraviolet radiation, which broke down the bonds between carbon molecules.

With a nod, Rick said, "That's fine. Good thinking, Doctor. You too, Joe. Zack, take a small gun in hand. Carry something better with you. Just in case."

The Marine lieutenant stood at attention, saluted, and said, "Yes, sir!" He put the rifle down and put a strap on his back to hold the larger gun, then picked up a .45 caliber pistol. It was powerful for a weak weapon, but Nancy could tell it still disgusted him.

They waited for Walker to return from the hospital with specimen jars and collecting devices. Joe found it difficult to snap the suit closed at the waist since he could not see it, and all the practice on their journey here had not helped him much. "Again, I'm sorry I take so long," he said. "I wish I knew what the problem is."

About a minute later, Walker returned and finished getting into his suit. Once the doctor was finished, Rick raised his hand to draw everyone's attention. "Ladies and gentlemen," he said, "this is a momentous moment for all humanity." He pulled the lever to open the crew hatch.

Yolanda could feel everyone ogling over her shoulder at the vast sea of red dirt and brown rock. The monument known as the Face was behind them, leaving a vast desert in front of them, cut off by a low mountain range far in the distance. The satellite Phobos was crawling across the crimson sky, barely noticeable because of its small size and distance; only its rapid velocity let them know what it was.

Rick looked at the science expert and said, "Doctor Yolanda Flores, you have the honor."

Yolanda took a look at the ground beneath her, then stepped back to watch as Gary attached the rope ladder with steel rungs to the floor and let the end fall. It did not take long, but it was the most thrilling experience of her life aside from when she would set foot on the planet. She took a deep breath, turned around, and stepped onto the first rung. Slowly, she worked her way down the ladder until she was only a step above the ground. Looking down, she saw two fairly large rocks beneath her. She let go of the ladder and fell with her feet on either side of the rocks. She jumped when she heard cheering coming from her intercom, then looked up to see everyone applauding. "*¡Viva Mexico!*" This time she started dancing, causing a small dust storm.

As Captain Newman climbed down, Yolanda cleared the rocks to make a safe area for them all at the bottom. Walker followed the captain, his specimen-taking equipment strapped to his back. Zack dropped the rifle to Rick before climbing down, then took it back after he quickly reached the bottom. Adam was next, who immediately walked over to the dark gray inflatable wheels to see how they were doing. Nancy came next, and Joe stared into the distance, waiting for Walker to climb back with his samples, which only took a few seconds, before climbing down to the planet.

Rick looked around. "Adam, Gary," he said, "let's hook up the hose to the lander to refuel. The rest of you look around. There's bound to be something of interest to someone."

All the explorers began going separate directions. Rick, Gary, and Adam were the only ones to make a sound over their intercoms for a few moments, all of them discussing the operation at hand. Nancy followed Yolanda as she stepped around the front of the ship. As they looked at the sight that was now before them, the sight made them both emit a loud gasp. Everyone looked in their direction to see that they had both stopped mid-stride, staring at whatever was behind the ship. Running over, each of them in turn did exactly the same as she had.

Not far behind the shuttle, previously unseen because of the oversized wheels, were three pyramids. One had collapsed on its side, but the steps leading to the flattened top on the foremost one were still intact. "It looks like the ones in Mexico," Yolanda commented.

"That one's Egyptian," Joe said. Nancy looked at him to see that he was looking at the one in the middle. Indeed, it was once perfectly sloped with no obvious means of entry except for a small, almost invisible gap in the center about twenty feet above the ground. The top was flat, like the Great Pyramid of Khufu at Giza. The last was a step pyramid, which Nancy recognized from a description Joe told her while talking to them about pyramids. It was built as a series of steps, each about twenty feet above the other. Only one existed on Earth, one of the first pyramids built in southern Egypt.

Nancy closed her eyes in disbelief, then opened them again. She turned away, slowly began wandering, and said, "I can't believe this. It has to be circumstance."

"What do you think, Commander?" asked Gary. "Do you think this is the proof?"

Rick took two steps forward and eyed the structures for a few moments, seemingly impervious to the shock everyone else was feeling. He then looked to the enormous monument to their left. "Look," he said, pointing.

The "face" had what appeared to be hieroglyphs of iron embedded into the rock. A downward arrow, a group of people, an eye, an outline of some kind. All three repeated each other around the base of the monument. Even Nancy began doubting her own self-determined purpose. "This is impossible," she said. "But there it is." She tried not to babble and held herself to, "How is this possible?"

Joe went over to her and put his hand on the shoulder of her suit. "Only one of us could be right," he said. "I'm sorry." He looked up toward the flight deck. Nancy looked up instinctively to see Walker staring out the side of the window trying to get a good look at what they saw.

As the rest of them began looking at each other in awe, Rick turned and said, "Mister Rommel, Doctor Flores, Lieutenant Knight, you come with me. Doctor Villareal, help Mr. McCrone and Commander Singh refuel the ship."

"Roger," Nancy said as she turned to the tube with the others, more than happy to get away from the vision of the structures.

Joe knew that Nancy did not appreciate doing an engineer's work, but they both understood that the few of them would be unable to answer all the new questions in the little time they had. Sacrifices had to be made if they were going to investigate the pyramids and there was little else they could do.

It took twenty minutes to reach the pyramids. Up close, it was as if they were built as duplicates of the pyramids on Earth. They agreed that the Aztec style pyramid, the one with a stairwell, looked too dangerous to investigate, but the Egyptian one was still in fairly good shape. They climbed the side to the entrance and found a shaft sloping upward just enough to necessitate a small amount of work by anyone walking.

"How far would you say it is up there?" Rick asked.

Joe turned on a light on the arm of his suit and shone it up the shaft. "It looks like it's a long way," he said. "If it's the same as the Great Pyramid, it won't be too far and there should be some side shafts."

Yolanda and Rick turned on their lights to amplify what Joe was producing. In the distance, they could just see what appeared to be a stone wall marking the end. "About four hundred feet," commented the commander. Joe and Yolanda nodded in agreement.

Rick shone his light on the floor. "Ridges," he said. "Looks like someone actually used this place and didn't want anyone to fall." He cautiously stepped in and began making his way upward, Joe following, and Yolanda behind him. As Zack started to enter, Rick stopped him by saying, "Lieutenant, you stay here. Watch and warn us if anything happens."

"Yes, sir!" came the loud response. Joe thought he heard a hint of disappointment in the Marine's voice.

They carefully strode up the shaft, noting the rugged, worn down rock around them. Much like in Egypt, Joe thought. Yolanda appeared to be simply amazed. The occasional look at each other was a good break from the tension.

They reached the end about a minute later and looked around. "It doesn't look like there's anything here," Yolanda said. "It's just a small chamber."

They had entered a small, rectangular chamber about twenty feet wide. Reddish rock with green specks filled the walls, one near the entrance larger than the others. The floor was the same as the passage, while the ceiling seemed to be made out of small, red pebbles. As Joe searched for anything unusual, he noticed a crack at the bottom of the wall across from the entrance about three feet wide and a quarter of an inch high. He then looked at the wall that the area marked off and noticed a symmetrical outline. "Captain," he said, "it looks like there may be a door here."

Stepping forward, Yolanda looked at it. "It does," she agreed. "It looks like it may have swung outward at some point." She directed her light downward to look at the small billows of dust their feet were creating. "It has been a very long time."

"Probably millennia," Joe added.

Just then, Gary's seemingly distant voice came over the intercom, saying, "Commander?"

Rick's attention perked as he answered, "Yes?"

"We've finished the refuel," Gary said. "We have two hours if we're going to assure reaching Jupiter as planned since we were behind schedule arriving here, and we need to clear a path for takeoff just in case. We've already started, but I had to use the ship's radio to contact you."

"Acknowledged," said Rick. He turned to the others. "Does this look man-made to you?"

Joe turned to the cavern. "Artificial, yes," he said. "Whether it's man-made or not is a subject for debate. There's still a lot we don't know."

Looking closely at the walls, Yolanda said, "I believe it may be natural, but I may also be wrong. There have been many sandstorms on this planet and these walls appear to have been eroded by small, abrasive particles. The only sign that it could be artificial is that it appears to have been perfectly straight long ago."

Joe thought a moment and turned to the others. "Doctor Flores, can you explain how so many sandstorms would not do great damage to those ridges along the walkway, or disturb those symbols outside?"

Yolanda stared at him blankly for a moment; obviously, she had no answer. They looked back to Rick to see him examining a small depression in the rock beside the possible door. "Let's go," the flight commander said. "We can't risk missing that fuel rocket at Jupiter." As they left, Joe thought he saw Rick slip something into the pocket of his space suit in the corner of his eye.

Back at the ship another twenty minutes later, Gary, Adam, and Nancy were clearing rocks to make a runway. Joe and Zack joined in while Rick and Gary checked the inflatable tires, which were in good shape for such a rough landing. An hour later, they had cleared a clear strip of land half a mile long in front of the ship. During the conversation, they found that less than half of the fuel in the lander was needed to resupply the Diablo. Everyone also kept a rock or two for souvenirs. Joe was fascinated by the one Nancy chose: a bluish, almost perfectly round rock that looked out of place on this now-barren world.

They returned to the ship and climbed to the hatch, then returned to their seats. Adam's investigation of the inflatable wheels showed that there was a possible danger, but clearing the runway was given as the main reason why there was no problem during take-off.

Chapter Six

Thirteen weeks after leaving Mars, Nancy was having very disturbing dreams. They had started after Rick had let her pilot the ship past a rather large asteroid, only to come close to slamming into another one hidden behind it. The second asteroid was rather small and she had missed by several hundred feet, but the fear of nearly killing them all still held firmly to Nancy's mind. She later determined that the smaller asteroid was orbiting the larger, and they decided to stay farther away from any other asteroids they might encounter.

That near-disaster was foremost on her mind when she awakened that day. As always, Joe was munching on a food bar in his skivvies while tending to the plants they depended upon so greatly for oxygen and occasional relief from the boringly monotonous food bars. She pulled herself out of her mattress without him hearing and floated over to him, leaving her cooling-ventilation garment behind.

As she wrapped her arms around his waist, he involuntarily jerked free and yelped. Once he regained his composure, he turned to her and said, "Sorry, Nancy. I'm a little jittery. They didn't tell us the asteroids would be this concentrated. We're spotting one every other hour, and we've even discovered three."

Nancy was slightly amused at the news. "So what's going on?" she asked as she nervously drifted to retrieve her suit.

"Not much," Joe answered. "The only thing that may be significant is that Yolanda and I were examining the rock you picked up. It's real fascinating. It doesn't look like it belonged on the planet."

Nancy laughed and said, "That's why I picked it up. I wanted to study it and show it was natural." Curiosity intrigued her at that moment. She stopped as she was about to put on her suit and asked, "What happened?"

"It scared us," said a female voice behind her that startled the over-exposed astrophysicist. To the surprise of both of the old friends, Yolanda had been watching them. "We were doing a birefringence test, and for an instant the entire rock just...flashed." Much to Joe and Nancy's surprise, Yolanda pulled herself out of the bunk to reveal she also had a habit of slipping her suit off in her bunk. She did not seem to care that Joe and possibly Rick could see her, but Nancy did and gave Joe a quick look that stole her love interest's attention. "I could not sleep after that," the mineralogist added as she began reaching for her cool-ing-ventilation garment, partly using her legs in a manner that even Nancy would not dare with him.

"Can we repeat it?" Nancy asked, eager to learn more about the specimen she had randomly found, but gave Joe a look that made him avert his eyes because she had not been asked. It was not so much her question, but the presence of a second beautiful, sexy, and—most importantly—completely naked woman in his presence.

Yolanda began putting her suit in mid-air as Joe said, "Recreating the conditions won't be hard at all. I was turning it, though, and we don't know if that was part of what happened."

Joe led the way into the space lab, where Yolanda moved two of the intense plant lights from the ceiling to the table. As she set them facing each other, Nancy retrieved her rock from where Joe had returned it. She noticed it was a curious specimen, appearing as if it had once been spherical and worn down by the almost constant sandstorms the planet experienced, as she pulled it out of her storage compartment. The two had created a vice out of a pair of tongs, some gauze, and a rubber band, which Yolanda placed the rock inside and secured with the gauze-cov-ered tongs. She then set up the two lights so they faced each other, the specimen between them. "Are you sure this will work again?" she asked

"No," said Joe, "but we can sure try." He turned off the lights to the space lab as Yolanda turned on the two lights positioned on opposite sides of the rock. "For a moment, I thought it exploded when it happened," he added while floating around to look at it from different angles.

The purpose of the test was to see what colors reflected in which directions. As Joe and Nancy both floated around the rotating rock, it seemed to change from blue and green to white and brown to black and orange to purple and yellow. It was a test Nancy had done in chemistry class, but all she knew for sure was that the lack of dark red areas showed there was no rust. Yolanda stayed in one place, near the seat where she could easily reach both the main light switch and the testing lights, which she recognized had been moved from giving necessary light to the plants. "You're really fascinated with my rock," she said.

Yolanda took a quick glance at her and said, "We were just taking a quick look at it since it was so different. We weren't expecting this." A few moments passed by before she added, "When we looked at it under the electron microscope, it looked like it was actually changing colors."

They hovered for several minutes in total silence, staring at the orb-like object in front of them. "Nothing," Joe finally said. "It's not doing anything out of the ordinary."

"You said you were turning it," Nancy said. "Do you remember how?"

Joe and Yolanda both looked at it quizzically before the science officer took two pens and began turning it in place with surprising skill. "Remember what you said?" Joe asked.

This seemed to trigger a memory in Yolanda. She moved it to a specific position, made sure it was right, and said, "Here goes." She began rotating it to her right along the axis created by the tongs. An instant later, it suddenly gave off a brilliant flash of blue light that seemed to fill the space lab. They all gave out quick screams before realizing what had happened, causing Yolanda to knock the item of their investigation free. Nancy caught it just before it struck a control panel, turning her body to reduce the effect of the specimen's inertia.

They all looked at each other for a few moments before Nancy handed it back to Yolanda to repeat the procedure. Again, the specimen flashed. This time they were not as startled. "Try holding it there," said Nancy.

Joe looked at Yolanda and said, "It's worth another shot." The statement was obviously meant to let Nancy know without being rude that they had tried it before. Yolanda repeated the procedure with remarkable slowness and stopped the instant the flash occurred, but it faded as quickly as it appeared.

"Nothing," said Nancy. "I've found something out of place, it turns out to be out of the ordinary, and now I'm starting to think we're out of our minds."

Yolanda smiled at her and said, "We'll find it. You found this by accident, we found this property of it by accident, but it was no accident that it repeated. We'll find it."

Still half-doubtful, Nancy said, "Most scientific discoveries are the result of accidents."

Joe leaned in close to the rock. "Look at it" he said. "Does it look like it's glowing to you?" Indeed, it did. The light was causing a very faint glow inside the rock. Nancy knew the look in her eyes confirmed it as well as Yolanda's Spanish whisper to God.

As Yolanda reached down to turn it to a different angle, the unusually frightened voice of Commander Newman came screaming from the flight deck, "What in the world is that?" They forgot the rock as the potential horrors of the asteroid belt roared through their minds and quickly moved through the mid deck toward the flight deck.

When they arrived, they found Zack flying through the access, still in his sleepware, rifle already in hand. Nancy became convinced at that point he slept with it. "What's going on?" Nancy demanded as they arrived.

Rick pointed out the window to space and nervously said, "There. They just started appearing a moment ago."

Nancy looked out to see that the sky definitely looked very different. Indeed, many more stars were present. She was startled when she suddenly noticed that one was actually moving. Another was, as well. And another. Several. Many. Soon, the sky was filled with moving stars. No, not stars. They were getting bigger. After a few seconds, a chill ran through her as she realized that she was staring at a fleet of craft they did not recognize. She was the only one able to make any sound, but only a gurgle came out of her throat. Rick was the first to regain his composure, turning to Gary and saying, "Turn us around. It looks like our mission is about to be aborted."

Gary turned the ship one hundred eighty degrees on the yaw as everyone braced against the wall. Before they had finished revolving, they could see another set of ships beginning to close in from the other direction, identified only by their shadows against the sun. "We're trapped between them," Zack said. "They're heading straight for each other. We may have stumbled upon a battlefield."

Rick turned to Gary and asked, "Can we get out of the kill zone?"

"No," was the pilot's answer. "There are too many of them, and they're closing in too fast."

Joe threw up his arms, causing him to spin backward as Nancy looked on in horror. "Great," he said. "What do we do now?"

On the verge of sheer panic, Adam asked, "What would happen if we found ourselves in the middle of a battle? They won't recognize this ship! They'll blast it for sure! We're out here in the middle of nowhere! And the first ones we meet out here will kill us! We'll be the first people to die in space!"

"It looks like Adam's right this time," said Rick as he seemed to begin preparing to offer up a speech in his mind.

Joe froze for a moment after stopping his rotation and proclaimed, "That's it! Adam's right, but that's how we could survive!"

"How?" The word came from Adam's tense mouth, while everyone else listened in the faint hope that the parapsychologist was right.

"We're not with either group, we didn't make a hostile move, and we have a different ship design," Joe answered. "In fact, we tried to run. If we look like we're not hostile then maybe they can tell we're not with them. Maybe they'll let us fly right through them to safety."

A few tense moments went by as they considered the situation. "Let's hope so," said Rick. "Pray. Captain, continue course for Jupiter, but be careful of those ships."

"Yes, sir!" Gary proclaimed as he spun the ship back around to see the ships had almost reached them. One was almost directly in front of them, and Nancy felt pangs of horror; however, the oncoming ship altered its course at the last moment and went past them. Other ships also veered away as they approached, taking no hostile action.

They all took a good look at the ships as they passed. They were about a kilometer long, pointed with three visible engines, more like pods, that ejected a thin transparent stream that quickly seemed to disappear into the vacuum. They touched the edge of one and felt the Diablo lurch to a slightly faster velocity. A wide window was at the front of each of the oncoming vessels, but they passed by too quickly to see the occupants. Once they finished passing the fleet, Rick said, "Turn us around. I want to see what's going on."

"You're not the only one," Gary muttered loudly as he began the turning procedure. As they turned, they saw flashes of light appearing, dust and debris quickly accumulating into what looked more like a darkly colored cloud speckled by sporadic red, yellow, and orange flashes masking the distant sun as they continued to move further away. The two opposing forces had, indeed, engaged in combat.

Confronted with the final decisive evidence that her ideals had been wrong, Nancy could watch no more and began moving back through the mid deck and into the space lab. As she reached the interdeck access, Walker tilted over to her and asked, "Are you all right, Nancy?"

"I'm fine," she said. "I'm just frustrated over all this, that's all."

The doctor leaned over and offered her a mild sedative, which she declined as she continued on her way. Once back in the space lab, she spotted her rock in the intense lights and moved to look at it to try to take her mind off what she had just seen. It seemed almost alive, the reflecting surface changing with the different ways she looked at it. Over all, it looked ocean blue with green flecks in the light, almost like a water planet mottled by islands. The blue areas shone from certain angles in the light, almost like a dimly lit light bulb, while the green areas gave no such reflection and allowed no light to penetrate.

She placed her eyes close to the sample and stared at it in the bright lights. When it appeared blue and green, it reminded her of where she had come from, and for the first time she felt homesick. She had been so exited about proving what she had always believed to be true, and now there was so much evidence that she was wrong that she now knew she had no choice but to surrender. It was the one purpose she felt she had in life, and now it was impossible for her to continue.

She turned off the light so she could see it without the shine. It looked as dull as a normal rock without the intense light, though still oddly colored. This was what she saw when she first picked it up while clearing the runway: a simple rock that formed from the magma of the volcanoes that dotted the Martian landscape long ago. Now, it was a symbol of her failure. She had succeeded at everything she knew she had to do to accomplish her given task. Now that task was a failure, and that made her a failure. She thought she was beginning to understand Adam.

The ship began rotating to point forward again as she was about to let herself drift to the ceiling in misery, forcing her to quickly move to avoid being hit by the wall. It was like dodging the ships they had just encountered, only she was the ship and the wall was the fleet. She wished she was back home where she would still be ignorant of this hard truth. A few moments later, she heard a hand softly hit the wall behind her, and from the otherwise silent approach she knew who it was. "I'm all right, Joe," she said. "I just need to get used to this, that's all."

Her childhood friend moved in front of her and looked her in the eye. "We're not going back yet," he said. "The rest of us want to, but Rick points out that we're supposed to look for life on the Gallilean moons, too. He's right, and the rest of us know it. We don't know who that was, and since this is happening in our star system we have to. We don't know what the third assignment is, either. It looks like we weren't told what it is so you wouldn't make a big deal out of it with the media. It was bad enough as it was. You saw the protesters."

Nancy glided back down onto the floor, half-wishing she was wearing magnetic boots to ground her. "It looks that way," she said. "I guess we'll find out. I just know I was wrong." She looked up sadly at him. "It couldn't be testing the engine." Inside, she had horrid suspicions centered on some of the stories Joe told her that she had dismissed as fantasy in the past.

Joe stroked her face and said, "Don't worry. It couldn't be anything serious." A moment passed as they just looked at each other, suddenly lost in a brief moment of weakness. Joe began slowly leaning in her direction, and she did not mind. For the first time, she felt more than friendship from him. She began leaning toward him as well, and knew that the time had come that she had hoped for years would—

A soft thud and a muffled cry broke the mood. They looked over at the source of the sound to see Walker and Yolanda trying to untangle from each other while they tried to stop spinning. After a moment, they finally regained themselves and Yolanda smiled. "Sorry!" she loudly whispered as she turned to leave.

Joe and Nancy moved slightly away from each other, Nancy losing her balance and spinning away, unseen by the turning Joe. "No, I should be going back up front," said Joe. Nancy saw him turn to look at her just as she hit the ceiling.

Chapter Seven

Almost four weeks had passed since they had encountered the alien fleet, and nothing significant had happened since. They only considered two events important. One was a course correction which was blamed on the push everyone felt as they went through what they assumed had been exhaust from the alien engine and debris from the battle passing a few miles away. The other was the ability to study part of one of the alien ships as debris from the battle passed by a few miles away. A questioning optimism was beginning to take hold inside the ship, the optimism being led by Walker and the questioning being led by Adam. That optimism was caused mainly by the realization that Jupiter had been steadily growing for several days. In fact, the larger moons had been visible for the last few hours. The questioning was what dangers there could have been, especially now that one great mystery of the universe had been decisively answered.

Everyone except Rick and Joe floated in the flight deck looking at the vision of the enormous world, which was more astounding than they expected. They watched as they passed the tiny satellite Carme. It was not the outermost satellite, but it was the first one they would pass.

Joe arrived on the flight deck to find Nancy in the pilot's seat and Walker behind her, both amazed at the sight. "Incredible, isn't it?" the physician asked.

"It sure is," Joe answered.

Nancy added, "Even Rick was amazed by it, and he never seems to be fazed by anything."

Almost as if on cue, the commander drifted through the hatch from the mid deck. "Wow, we're close," he said as he looked outside. "I'll take over, Nancy."

As she unfastened herself from the seat, Nancy eyed a light moving ever so slightly that indicated the next satellite they would pass. "I'll see where our target is," she said and maneuvered to the computer console. She brought up the graphic of the locations of the satellites, but found something else. She took a quick look out the window, then rechecked her findings. "Commander," she said, "do you see where that moving light is ahead?"

"Yes," Rick answered. "What about it?

Nancy looked at the flight commander and said, "According to the computer, there's nothing there."

Rick and Gary looked at each other in surprise. They smiled and Gary said, "Sounds like a new satellite."

"Maybe not," Joe said. "After all we've seen so far, it could be anything."

As Adam entered behind Joe, Rick said, "Let's check it out. Gary, would you do the honors?"

"I'd be glad to," the pilot responded as he set the controls. A moment later, he began maneuvering the craft to gradually move in the direction of the object.

A few minutes later, as they were approaching, Nancy sat up straight as a tree with a start and said, "That's not a satellite." It was a statement, not a guess.

"You're right," Joe confirmed.

Rick and Gary continued looking straight ahead while the others looked at the astrophysicist. "What makes you so sure?" Rick asked.

Nancy moved forward in the cabin to point as she spoke. "It's not in a proper orbit," she said. "It's too far out of the plane of orbit and it's also moving retrograde to the other satellites."

"Could you explain that, please?" asked Walker.

Nancy obliged, "That means it's orbiting in the wrong direction. Anything that orbits moves in the same direction the object it's orbiting rotates in. This is going the other way. It's also at too much of an angle to the others. No satellite has that much of an angle to its orbit. Look, it's too small, too."

By this time, Joe had returned from the mid deck with the binoculars. All of them stared as they approached. Each of them gasped in shock as they took the binoculars. It was a ship not unlike the ones that had appeared in front of them a few days after leaving Mars, except it was considerably smaller and appeared to have sustained a vast amount of damage to most of it. One side had a gaping hole, exposing what appeared to be rooms and corridors. It was darkened, and there was no indication of any activity on board.

Rick turned to Gary. "Can you park us next to that ship?" he asked.

"Yes," Gary answered. "I can bring us within a few feet, but with how slow it's moving, it's orbit will decay in no time."

Several moments passed as Gary prepared to turn the ship around and began a deceleration burn. Joe was already heading to the mid deck to put his suit on, saying, "This is what I'm here for."

Walker followed him down the ladder. "There may be someone still alive in there," he said. "If there is, we'll need each other's help."

"I'll go with you," said Rick. "This could be first contact. They may want to speak with the commander of this vessel." As he climbed down the ladder, he added, "Joe, you're the expert on ETs. Do you know how to handle a situation like this?"

As he grabbed his space suit, Joe said, "In my occupation, I run the risk of having a first contact situation. I've run the scenario in my mind hundreds of times. I know what to do in theory, but in practice…" There was no need to bring up the fact that no such practice had been needed since the Conquistadors, so he simply shrugged to complete that part of his thought. "It all depends on their culture."

Rick nodded as he slid into the pants of his space suit and said, "I'm placing you in charge of any contact we may have. You're probably the only one with any idea what to say. Any of the rest of us could cause a conflict we don't want. Adam, get down here and suit up. I want you to take a look at that ship and see if you can figure out what happened."

"Yes, sir," came the engineer's shaky voice from the flight deck.

"Lieutenant Knight," Rick continued, "we'll need you."

"Yes, sir!" said the weapons expert as he flew down face first from the flight deck. "Right away, sir!"

The commander finished, "The rest of you stay here. Doctor Licht, Mr. McCrone, and Mr. Rommel are the only ones going. If something happens, it's up to you to complete the mission."

Captain Singh loudly said, "Yes, sir," through the intercom from the pilot's seat. They could also hear Nancy saying something unkind that had been meant to be out of their earshot, followed by laughter.

After several minutes, Gary stopped the ship some fifty feet from the alien ship, an ever so slight drift almost unnoticeable. The party entered the airlock from the space lab, from which the air was evacuated. The hatch then opened to allow them to fly to the derelict ship with ease. They flew their suits to the gap in the hull, finding a partially open door leading inside. "Help me," said Rick. Together, the five of them pried open the door just wide enough for them to pass through.

Once inside, they found smooth, red walls with wide blue stripes on the ceiling every few feet. Bodies littered their path, floating in the hallway. As Joe floated past them along the ceiling, he took a close look at the stripe and said, "It looks like this entire wall...ceiling...everything is in one piece. My guess is that somehow this blue part of the ceiling produced light before this crate was put out of commission."

Walker moved to the closest body and looked at it with his wrist light. Joe could tell that rigor mortis had set in, and it was difficult to tell what it may have been like while alive. From Walker's eyes, Joe knew that one thing was unmistakable. The doctor looked at his crew mates and pronounced, "He's human."

"Human?" repeated Zack as he floated to set himself next to Walker. "Are you sure?"

Walker looked over the body again. "The face, skin, even the way rigor mortis set in. He's definitely human."

Joe remained unconvinced. "You may not be able to tell from just looking," he responded. "You have to see if there's the slightest difference." He started to reach for the being's clothing, but stopped nervously at the thought of handling a dead body. "Maybe you should do this."

"Hold it," said Rick. "Zack, can you take it back to the ship and get back here quickly?"

The Marine looked directly at the commander and carefully considered the consequences of his next words. "Sir," he said, "I may of more use here. If there are any survivors, they could be hostile and I would be needed."

Rick looked at the bodies. "No. They're too human, and there are too many holes in this ship. Take the body back to the Diablo." Disappointed, Zack gave his acknowledgment and began moving the body.

The rest of them hovered in the long hallway. They looked around for the first time and realized the door they came through once led to a small room that was now somewhere in space, probably in small, unrecognizable pieces. There was no indication of power, and the hall went several hundred feet in either direction. "Let's split up," Commander Newman said. "It looked like the rear was that way. Adam, you come with me." He looked at Joe and Walker. "You two find the command center and see what you can do."

"Yes, sir," Joe and Walker both said. Turning, they headed to the front of the ship. The corridor turned sharply to the right at the end, continued to the midline of the ship, then branched to the front. After a couple of minutes, they found a door with inscriptions upon it in an indecipherable language. Nonetheless, Joe recognized the inscriptions. "My God," he said in awe.

Walker turned to him, then back to the door, asking, "Do you recognize it?"

Rick's voice came over the intercom, asking, "Have you found something, Mister Rommel?"

"Yes," Joe answered. "We may have found a door leading forward and it has what appears to be writing in an alien script on it."

Walker added, "It's unintelligible, whatever it is. Just a bunch of lines, curves, and circles, all intersecting each other."

Before Rick could make a comment, Joe jumped in and said, "Sir, they're identical to a crop circle that was found in England some years ago."

"*Saaaaay what?*" It was the first unprofessional thing any of them had heard Commander Newman say in the past seven months. Joe could have sworn the flight commander sounded scared.

Joe described, "It's basically two circles side by side connected by a horizontal line between their centers. To the left are two arcs concentric with the left circle, one above the other. The right circle has a cross through it making up part of the line connecting them. There's a dot in the upper right quadrant of that circle. That's it."

Several moments passed by before Rick said, "Diablo, are you hearing this?"

Gary's voice answered, "Yes, but none of us are sure we believe it."

Walker said, "I can confirm it. It's right here in front of us." After a very brief pause, he added, "I'm still not sure I believe it, either."

A brief pause prompted the question Joe felt needed to be asked. "We're at the front of the ship, and this door is closed. It probably leads to whatever passes for a bridge here. Diablo, can you see if it's been hit?"

"Not from where we are," came Gary's voice. "We can maneuver there if you want."

Before Gary finished speaking, a red glow appeared behind them. A moment later, the door opened to allow a very soft breeze to hit their suits. Beyond was a fairly large bridge with an enormous window in front, giving a spectacular view of the world below. "Diablo," Joe cautiously said, "I don't think that will be necessary. It looks like we just received an invitation."

Several tense moments went by before Rick slowly said, "Uh, Joe, could you repeat that?"

Joe glanced at Walker and said, "The door just opened for us. I think there's an atmosphere. It's being held in, possibly by this red glow that showed up behind us. It must be some kind of force field. I'm entering."

Almost immediately, Nancy voice came over the intercom. "Be careful," were her only words.

They entered and looked around. At the front was an enormous, convex window from which one could look more than ninety degrees in either direction. From the view, Joe concluded that the console in the window was for a pilot or navigator. Numerous consoles in two semicircles surrounded the room, leaving the rear open and empty. Several of the consoles had exploded or melted. Burned and battered bodies were everywhere.

Joe looked at one of the damaged consoles on the outside of the bridge and spotted a bright bluish-yellow glow. "Doctor Flores, are you there?" he asked.

"I am here," came the soft voice with the Spanish accent.

Joe peered into the console and asked, "I need to know something. There's a visible short circuit in a panel that looks like it exploded. There's a very small flame, but not big enough to indicate a lot of oxygen. Can an electrical fire burn anything other than oxygen?"

A moment went by as Yolanda thought about it. "What color is the flame?" she asked

"Yellow with a blue base," answered the paranormal investigator.

Yolanda answered, "It sounds like it is burning oxygen. It also means the ship has not been drifting long. If someone is still alive, it may burn up everything it is living on right now. Do you see anything to put it out with?"

Joe looked around, then at Walker, who shrugged. "No," Joe replied. "Just my fingers."

Again, the crackle of the radio indicated Yolanda was about to speak. "Do it," she said. "Quickly. We don't want to melt the fingers of your suit, but we don't want the fire to spread, either. If it burns through your glove, the oxygen in your suit will explode if you're lucky." There was no need to tell him about what would happen if his suit ruptured in the vacuum of space.

Walker floated over to Joe's location just in case the investigator needed him. "I'm here, Joe. Go for it."

"No," Joe answered. "If the suit explodes, we don't need to lose you, too. Get over there." He pointed to the other side of the room.

Walker looked at him solemnly for a moment before Rick's voice said, "I concur with Mr. Rommel. Get clear, Doctor."

As Walker acknowledged him and went back to the egress, Joe looked at his gloved hand and offered a silent prayer. If there was a time to be glad to know God, it was now. Once Walker was safely away, Joe made up his mind, suddenly reached into the panel, grabbed the flame, and immediately let go. Checking to see what he had done, he said, "It's out." He looked at his hand. "My glove started to get warm, but it isn't melting. I'm all right." Joe and Walker looked at each other in relief.

A few moments later, Adam uncertainly said, "I've found what looks like a main console for the engineering section. There are crop markings that look like these crop circles Joe described on it, too. I can't make heads or tails of anything else."

Zack's voice came over the radio next. "Sir, I'm back from the Diablo. I'm heading to the bridge."

"No," Joe interrupted. "Whatever's keeping the air from getting out probably won't let you in."

"Sir?" Zack inquired.

A few pregnant moments went by before Rick said, "I agree," the captain answered. "There's nothing you can do."

A moment went by before Zack disappointedly answered, "Yes, sir. Of course."

"We could use you back here," Rick added. "I've found what I believe to be a weapons system. I'd like you to take a look at it."

"Yes, sir!" Zack replied enthusiastically.

As Rick, Adam, and Zack continued on, Joe continued looking at the shattered panel. "If it was burning a long time," said Joe, "there must be an oxygen supply."

Walker turned to him suddenly and said, "Don't do it, Joe. You don't know what germs could be on this ship."

"I know," Joe said, "but I think I can get more done if I took off my helmet. I heard you when you hit that panel floating over here, so there must be air. I'd be able to hear and smell and that would give me a better sense of what may have happened here."

Rick heard and firmly said, "Negative. Do not remove your helmet. If this is an alien ship, it may only take one germ to kill all of us."

Joe sighed. "With all due respect, sir," he replied, "as the crew's paranormal expert, I know the danger, but I don't think there is any danger. This ship is small, and judging from how everyone is burned, I don't think there's any chance of disease. Plus, it's now obvious that they've been interacting with us for years and there haven't been any suspicious outbreaks. Besides, if we do have a first contact, I don't want to try communicating though a piece of plastic."

Several moments went by. "All right," Rick finally said, "go ahead. Just be careful, Mr. Rommel."

Rick and Walker both slowly moved their hands up to remove their helmets. A brief look at each other, and they released the seals to their helmets. As they lifted them off, a slight stench of scorched bodies and burned out wiring struck them in contrast to the pure oxygen atmosphere they had been breathing. Both of them began gagging, prompting everyone else to demand what was happening. "It's just the smell," said Walker. "There's smoke from where Joe put out the fire, and there was apparently enough air to pick up the smell from all these bodies."

They stopped coughing enough to hear a soft, almost inaudible hissing. They both tracked it to the panel they were in front of and saw the source of the hiss. "It looks like we've found the source of the oxygen," said Walker. "There's a leak in the inner hull just inside the damaged panel and there's a canister on the other side. It's leaking."

"Be careful," said Yolanda. "The slightest spark could be disastrous."

Joe looked around and listened carefully. "I hear another leak." As he tried to track it down, he listened more carefully and realized, "That's no leak.". He slowly drifted to the front of the bridge where the sound was coming from, where the pilot's console sat inside the curved window. From there, Jupiter loomed seemingly larger than life.

It was what they found behind the console that drew their attention. A being was still trying to move, but his legs had been lost. He looked up at them in agony, amplified by heavy wheezing. This was it. First contact. Joe's could feel his heart racing and knew Walker's was doing the same.

Joe carefully walked over and kneeled down beside the being. "Commander," he said, "I've found a living, um, male. It looks human. He's lost his legs and there's blood everywhere."

"I can't save him with the equipment we have," said Walker. "I think he knows it."

Joe calmly took the being's hand in his still warm glove. "My name is Joe Rommel," he said. "I'm with the first human manned deep space expedition. Can you tell me what happened?"

For a moment, Joe thought the other space traveler was dead. Then the being slowly looked up and said, "No. Not...first. Many before. You...are tricked. Here to..." He winced. "Stop them. They...attacked us. They do...not...understand."

Concerned, Joe asked, "Who? Who attacked you?"

Desperately, the being said, "It was...the...Am...ericans.... Your own...people...do not...un...der...stand.... All we want...is..." His eyes glazed as his last breath left him.

Several moments went by in complete silence. Joe was still looking at the being in shock when he broke the silence. "What in the world...in the universe is going on?" He abruptly cut off his last word and said, "Did you hear that?"

"We heard it all," said Rick almost emotionlessly.

Gary chimed in, "So did we. Did he mean we're not the first humans to make it this far?"

Joe stood. "That's what it sounded like," he said. "Commander, do you have any idea what could be going on?"

"I only know what I've been briefed on," answered Rick. "Let's get back over to the Diablo. We still have a mission to complete."

In increasing annoyance, Nancy replied, "Sir, with this discovery, what is the point of continuing this assignment?"

With authority, the commanding officer said, "He said the Americans were responsible. That means the United States is at war with these beings and our mission may be to find alien bases and destroy them. Meet me at the opening immediately."

Joe and Walker exchanged glances. As they put their helmets back on, Joe said, "Yes, sir." As he started to leave, he turned back and asked, "Walker do you know which of these deactivates the force field?"

"I imagine it's the one that appears to be working," said the physician as he pointed to a light on the console they stood in front of.

"Oh?" Joe said with embarrassment, realizing he had overlooked the obvious. He pressed the button and the air suddenly rushed out of the bridge as the glow vanished, pulling them part of the way to the door. "Thanks," he said with embarrassment.

Chapter Eight

Nancy and Zack sat in the space lab playing their third game of chess to kill time. Nancy had lost the first two games, but this time she had him on the ropes. She had two extra pawns with nothing blocking their path, and they were each only two moves from becoming queens. Zack would have to bring his bishop back home to protect against the threat—or so she thought. Instead, he moved his rook to her end of the board to put her king in check. "Mate in five," he announced.

Shocked, she looked for a moment at the board before spotting the mating net. He had allowed the pawns to move forward and distract her from what he was doing. "Good game," she said as she tipped her king in defeat and extended her hand.

"Good plan," Zack answered as he accepted the proffered hand. "It would have worked if you moved your king to rook two first where your pawns protect it."

Nancy looked at the board one last time before putting the set away in its storage compartment. "I didn't really think it was a threat. I just missed the knight move that would have finished me off."

Just then, Joe peeked out from the hospital. "Walker's finished the autopsy," he said. "We want all of you there right away."

Nancy put up the chess set, wishing she could take a quick glance at Callisto as they gradually approached, while Zack went to call the others to the hospital. Once that was done, they went through the door to the hospital where the putrid scent of death from the decaying corpse struck them like an uppercut from a heavyweight champion. Walker stood in front of the covered body and Joe, who had assisted in the autopsy, moved beside him. Everyone but Captain Newman came to hear the results; someone needed to pilot the ship as they approached. Joe spoke first. "We found some very interesting results," he said, then turned the meeting over to the doctor.

Walker looked at the others with a very serious look that told them that he was about to say something most curious. "It looks human from all appearances," he began, "but it's not. If you care to see what I'm talking about, come forward. I'll describe it if you don't." He removed the cover from the body. Gary and Yolanda stepped forward. Nancy tried to peek into it from a distance out of curiosity. Zack and Adam both stayed back. All of them balked at the increased stench.

Walker continued, "If you know human biology, you know that the gall bladder produces bile. It's a small organ located next to the liver. But if you look at this being, there is no gall bladder. Instead, there's what I can only describe as a rock, and it's producing something, but it's not bile. It seems to be serving the same function, though. The blood is also slightly different." He held up two samples. "As you can see, their blood is more of a pinkish color than ours. I haven't isolated the exact reasons for these differences, yet."

He pulled the cloth back over the body before he continued, "As far as I can determine, this is normal for him. Except for this one organ and his blood, everything else is identical to our own. There may be less gastric fluid, but other than that it's the same."

Nancy finally managed with great reluctance to step forward and motioned for them to show her what Walker had discovered. The doctor responded, and Nancy looked into her first body cavity. She had a basic understanding of human anatomy and realized what he was talking about when she located the location of what should, by her logic, have been the gall bladder. The word "rock" seemed to her the best description, although not of any sort she had ever seen. "What does it mean?" she asked.

With a gesture, Doctor Licht motioned for Joe to take over the speech. "I think," the resident xenobiologist said, "this being may be closely related to us."

Several loudly quiet moments passed before Yolanda broke in and said, "I don't see how that could be possible."

"They're from a different place in the entire universe, Joe," Gary said. "How could they be our brothers and sisters?"

Joe drifted slightly upward into a position that made Nancy nervous. It was a position similar to one he usually took whenever he was going to make what she once assumed was insane conjecture. "There are several theories proposed, but only three make sense to me. One, held onto firmly by anthropologists, is that similar species develop along similar lines; however, they base this solely on culture, not biology. They site the worldwide occurrence of pyramids as evidence for this. The second is random chance, which is highly unlikely unless all life develops similarly, which is also unlikely."

"The third one is the one that bothers me," Nancy muttered to herself. "It always is." She did not care that she could be heard.

Joe settled into a chair, which was usually his mark of victory, and answered, "The third theory holds that long ago we traveled to the stars, then something happened: a catastrophe that put us back to the stone age."

With a start, Nancy remembered one thing Joe talked about often when they were growing up in New England. "Atlantis," she said. "A continent that was destroyed for reasons that nobody can agree on. Probably the one thing I would admit was possible before this trip began."

Nodding, Joe said, "Possibly. Atlantis, Lemuria, Mu…It's a strong possibility, if any of them are true. But if it is, then when this catastrophe occurred we were cut off from our own people."

"So why wouldn't they have helped us?" asked Zack.

Joe looked directly at the Marine and answered, "They may not have been able to help. Occupied somewhere else, maybe. Not able to get back in time, possibly. Distracted and unable to get back seems the most likely, based on our own history. By the time they returned, we'd forgotten about them or turned them into legends."

"And you think this is them?" asked Adam, fear strong in his voice. "It can't be right. We wouldn't make war on our own people."

Joe stood up and crossed through the air to the engineer. "Would we?" he asked. "Who else are we going to test new technology on?"

That comment upset Gary, who loudly said, "We just test it. We don't use people as guinea pigs."

"Sorry to disillusion you," Joe answered, "but I'm afraid we do. How else can we be so certain that everything works? We can't try it on other nations. When the first atomic bomb was tested, there was the fear that it would cause the entire atmosphere to combust. They didn't know if it would, and they detonated it outdoors anyway." The look on Gary's face told them that he was unaware of that historical potentially fatal, but obvious, mistake. "Don't put anything above anyone," Joe added. "They have some reason for fighting."

Several minutes went by as they hovered around the body, not caring about the stench that filled their lungs. Without a doubt, all of them were stunned by this possibility. Nancy found it difficult to admit to herself that it seemed the most likely.

It was finally Adam who broke the silence as he began fidgeting in midair. He looked as if he wanted to cry. "I once had a friend on the internet who was a computer hacker," he said. "She got a number from someone. I don't know who gave it to her, but it was the number to a top secret computer system. She was caught, but not before she put a number of files on disk and mailed it to me." He looked up, then down again. "It was a detailed accounting of known alien activity in our solar system. One of them talked about a war, but there were no details."

Joe pulled himself off the floor and floated over to Adam. "Wait a minute," he said, "was her name Bridget Saunders?"

"Yes," said the surprised engineer. "You knew her?"

Nancy interrupted, "Bridget Saunders? I thought her family moved."

"So we thought," said Joe. "The truth is, the entire family was arrested and everything in the house was confiscated because they never found what they were looking for. She got a message to me through someone who was released the next day. Just in time, too, since they were thrown into isolation. I have no idea what happened after that." He glanced at the horrified crew. "That's what drove me to enter this occupation." He looked at Adam. "Were you 'engine man at diamond world dot com?'" Adam looked at him in surprise and remembrance.

Everyone was gaping at the discovery. Nancy thought she could here Yolanda mutter, "So it's all true. But how?"

Joe let himself slowly fall back to the floor. Adam shook his head as he landed. "This isn't enough," the engineer said. "We have to get more to find out what's been going on."

Walker's grim demeanor was fractured by his voice. "I think I may be able to help," he said. "I had a practice near Kirtland Air Force Base three years ago. One day, something happened and they called me, asking me if I could come over to help. I only had one more patient, and when I finished with her, I went over there. I was told it was an accident with a grenade, and that's what it seemed to be. The damage showed it was an explosion, but as I was prepping him for the operation, he started babbling. I thought he was delirious at the time, but he said he was injured in space. Said that ships suddenly appeared where they were stationed and he was caught in an explosion when the base was hit."

Nancy stared at him, reeling. "Three years ago?" she asked with a level of timidity that rivaled Adam. For once, she did not care.

Walker looked at her and said, "Yes. April, to be exact. Why? Do you know something?"

Several moments passed as she looked around, then at Walker and said, "I think a colleague of mine may have seen the battle. I thought it was an intense meteor storm, but when I analyzed his data I couldn't figure out why the streaks were so short and went in different directions."

"I saw a crash that month," said Yolanda as she jerked up her head. "I was warned to say quiet, but I would not. Perhaps it was from that battle. I was living in northern Mexico, near Arizona. An American military group came for it."

This astounded everyone. "American?" asked Joe. "In Mexico?"

Yolanda nodded. "Villa Verde, to be exact."

"Yes," Joe said. "I'm very familiar with the case. I went down there a month later to investigate, myself, but all I found were people who wouldn't talk to me."

A smile broke onto Yolanda's face with a chuckle. "You must have just missed me. The local people finally chased me out. I lived in Monterey for a few months before moving to Mexico City."

The biggest surprise came from Zack. "I was on that squad," he said as he moved to avoid eye contact with Yolanda. "I questioned crossing the border, but I was quickly threatened with court martial to strictly obey orders and stay quiet about what I saw. It was definitely a ship. It wasn't like the ones we've seen so far. I didn't recognize it, but it had American markings." He turned to Joe. "I was the one who contacted MUFON about the case."

All attention turned to Gary. "Well," said Joe half-jokingly, "what's your story?"

Joe obviously did not expect an honest answer—Nancy knew his jokes well—but the pilot sighed and said, "Astronauts see UFOs close up on missions all the time. Rick has. I have. We never thought of it as anything special. It happens all the time. I assume you know that, Joe." The UFOlogist simply nodded with eyes the size of eggs. "Well, I saw the ship as it flew downward to Earth. I didn't know what it was because it was too far away, but it was after this not long after this battle that we seem to have discovered, here." He took a quick glance around. "And it was three years ago, in April."

"What the hell's going on?" Joe said with determination.

Suddenly, Captain Newman shouted for Commander Singh from the flight deck, sounding urgent. Alarmed, everyone raced forward to the flight deck to see what was causing the commotion. "What is it, Captain?" Gary asked as he led the way into the flight deck.

Rick took a quick glance at Gary and said, "Just started picking this up." He turned on the radio to reveal a series of long and short beeps. A pause. Three short. Three long. Three short. A classic S-O-S signal.

Rick turned the radio off as he said, "It seems that we may now know what our third assignment is. There's a downed American ship out here somewhere, and we are to find it and bring home any survivors." It did not seem right to Nancy. Wasn't one of the orders not to land? How could a downed crew survive for over half a year?

"Captain Singh," Rick said, "where is the signal coming from?"

Gary looked out at the planet and examined the data. After a moment he answered, "It's probably coming from the northern edge of Callisto, since it's so close and weak. Plus that area just came into view."

Rick turned to Zack and ordered, "Get the binoculars. I want some sign of where they are before we go down so we can conserve fuel. We're too low and we still haven't seen that fuel rocket." Nervous thoughts went through Nancy's mind before he added, "It must still be on the other side of the planet."

Time slowly passed as they moved into orbit of the frozen satellite. From below, Zack indicated the binoculars were coming their way and allowed them to float up, where Nancy distributed them. Everyone began looking for any sign of a crash. They looked over the large moon for twenty minutes before Yolanda finally said, "I see something. It's near the pole." Exactly where he said, Nancy realized.

"What does it look like?" Rick asked.

Yolanda glared at it for a moment. "Something is reflecting down there. It is very bright. I do not know of anything natural that could cause this on a world made of ice."

Rick dropped his binoculars. "I think we've found our men," he said. "Doctor Villareal, compute a course for descent."

"What about our orders?" asked Joe before Nancy could.

Rick looked back quickly and said, "Our orders allowed for exceptions. It seems at this point that we may have been meant to assist our men out here."

Nancy wondered why they would use such a long mission for rescue when it was obvious that they could send faster ships. She brought herself back to the present moment, turned to the computer, and input the information they had into a landing program, and found that the name of the valley was Gipul Carena. Two minutes later, it gave her a map showing everything they needed to know. "The computer says we need to take a longitudinal orbit and begin decelerating over the south pole. Counterthrust needs to be applied for four minutes thirteen seconds." She looked at the readout for several seconds in shock before saying, "There's a problem."

"What is that?" asked Rick.

Nancy turned forward and said, "Actually there are two problems. First is that the planet's surface is ice, so it's going to be very difficult to stop if we start sliding on it. The other one is the one I'm really worried about." She paused to get her breath. "There's no atmosphere." Why had they not been warned of this possibility during their training?

Both pilots looked back. "No atmosphere?" Gary repeated. "That means we're going to keep accelerating as we get lower."

A quick glance around showed her that the entire crew was in horror, thoughts running through their minds at a rapid pace. "What if we came down vertical, using thrust from the engines to slow our descent?" suggested Gary. "We'd level out at the last second."

Rick considered it for a moment. "It sounds good," he answered, "but those last few feet would have us accelerate. We'd need to be standing still when we begin leveling out at the last second to keep from doing serious damage to the wheels. Nancy, what would our ideal point of vertical thrust need to be and how high would we need to be to make sure we could turn to the horizontal in time?"

"Let me figure it out." Nancy input more numbers into the computer. A minute later, she came up with, "We would have to be six hundred feet above the ground, and we would land at—" her mouth stalled at the number in front of her. "Twenty-seven miles per hour," she finished. She then added, "We would have to use a deorbit burn of three minutes twelve point two seconds, and the vertical burn would be thirteen point one seconds, and we would have to start decelerating after thirty minutes and thirty-seven seconds."

Everyone exchanged glances, but she knew it was the best way to land if they wanted to be able to take off again. The decision was up to the flight commander. "Nancy," said Rick, "figure out our course. We begin decelerating as soon as possible."

Chapter Nine

As the others began preparing themselves for landing, Joe leaned over to Walker and whispered, "Join me in the hospital. I need to talk to you about something." A quick glance told him that Nancy had overheard him, but he motioned for her to stay put. The look on her face told him she had similar suspicions, or at least she knew what he was thinking.

Walker followed Joe reluctantly back to the hospital, the stench of the body still lingering like the unwanted houseguest that it was. Once they were safely inside, he asked, "Is something wrong?"

Joe closed the door and said, "Yes, there is." He floated near the door and made sure it was closed it to make sure they were not being overheard. "Have you paid special attention to Commander Newman?"

Surprised, Walker replied, "I haven't noticed anything unusual about him. Why do you ask?"

Letting himself slowly drift to rest against the starboard wall, Joe said, "There are a few things I've noticed, and as the onboard doctor, I assume you have some psychological training."

"Yes," said the medic. "Why?"

Joe spun and redirected himself near Walker, then spoke more quietly. "Some of the things he's done made no sense to me until earlier, when we found out about these experiences we've all had. Don't you think it's curious that all of us were put here together with this one thing in common?"

Walker shrugged and said, "Of course. I think we all noticed that. It's natural to be suspicious." He eyed Joe as he asked, "What's your take on all this?"

Staring Walker in the eye, Joe said, "We arrived here at Jupiter two days ahead of schedule, even possibly delayed by that attack fleet, using less fuel than we thought we'd need to."

"So?" the positive thinker demanded.

"So," answered the paranormal investigator, "when we were investigating those pyramids on Mars, he stopped Yolanda and me before we could even try to open a door we found, and he didn't even let Zack in when he could have possibly been of more use by staying with us. And when I looked at him just before we left, he was studying some depression by the door. Then he looked around on the ground and suddenly picked up a rock. Not any rock, the only one that didn't look like it was out of place. It looked like part of the ceiling fell off."

"What?" demanded Walker. "You think that's suspicious? Nancy did that, too. Joe, you're letting deep space get to you."

Not surprised, Joe moved back and said, "Just hear me out. Then if you still think I'm having problems, I'll do whatever you want."

Walker thought a moment. "Fine," he finally said. "Go ahead."

Joe took a deep breath. A moment later, he regained his composure and continued. "That alien told us that Americans attacked their ship, or at least they thought they were Americans."

"Wait a minute," Walker proclaimed as he held up his hands. "Are you trying to say that Commander Newman knew about this?"

Looking Walker straight in the eye, Joe answered, "He knows about something. Why didn't he take just five minutes to examine that depression and take more time on Mars if we had so much time left? The refuel rocket won't be visible for maybe a few more days. Given, with our technology we can go that far in a specific amount of time, so why did he want to leave right then?"

Walker looked at the alien body strapped to the table, then pulled out the two Mars rocks he had collected. Neither had an unusual color; both were brown, as expected. Nancy's was blue and green, however, and that well known among the crew as the source of Joe's doubts. Rick's translucent, round, red stone contributed. "Okay," Walker finally said, "I'll give you the benefit of the doubt. I'll wait until we see what we find down there before I pass judgment on you."

Suddenly the room began spinning. "The ship's turning around for deorbit burn," said Joe as they began swimming with the room. "We'd better go get ourselves strapped in."

They waited until the ship stopped rotating before they could safely reenter the flight deck. Nancy had already strapped in, while Zack, Yolanda, and Adam had returned to the mid deck. "We're going to begin deceleration in a few seconds," Gary said. "Strap in. Quickly."

"Adam?" Joe asked as Walker reached his seat, "what are you doing here?"

Adam's eyes showed terror as he said, "I didn't want to see it if something went wrong." Yolanda took the engineer's hand as Joe sighed and went to the flight deck.

Nancy smiled as Joe reached the flight deck and took Adam's seat. He secured himself quickly and Nancy hoped Walker had done so in time. "Beginning deceleration," proclaimed Gary, beginning the counterthrust just as Joe snapped his restraint in place. After one minute and thirteen seconds of inertia gently trying to pull them through the back of their seats, he said, "Done. We should be hitting the ground in thirty-three minutes."

"Please don't put it that way," said Joe. "Adam's worried enough as it is."

"I heard that!" a tense voice yelled from the mid deck as Joe fixed his helmet in place.

Nancy thought about Adam, wondering whom he was afraid they would find on the planet. He was nervous as usual, but this time she felt he had a right to be. Was Rick right in thinking that a rescue was the third assignment? Or was it a trap? Was this enemy actually sending out a deceptive signal to lure them into a trap? Or had an American ship actually crashed? Her thoughts drifted back to the battle-blasted alien ship they found. A few moments later, she forced her mind away from the damaged vessel and the morbid thoughts that came with it, letting it drift down to the seat next to her along with her eyes.

The wide, serious eyes of her closest friend on this journey told her all she needed to know. Whereas she had been waiting for this mission all her life, she had not anticipated anything going wrong with her plans. On the other hand, Joe had never dreamed of this, but it had ful-filled his every desire. She knew how elated he was over the events of the mission—everyone knew—and she could not help feeling happy, her-self. She was happy that Joe had finally found something to please him. Yolanda must have some excitement inside her, Walker was taking it very scientifically, and Adam must have been seeing visions of sudden, painful death going through his head, but none of their emotions could be as intense as Joe's must have been.

She tried to force herself not to cry, but a tear forced itself out any-way. A quick thought of Adam made her feel better that he had not seen it. This was not the time or place to explain, and she knew she would babble until Adam finally opened the crew hatch to jump out, probably killing them all in the process. She quickly wiped her eye and listened to the conversation between the commanders, remembering the landing on Mars and wondering how this would compare.

"We're approaching the deceleration point," Gary said. "I'm begin-ning the vertical maneuver."

Almost thirty minutes had passed by without Nancy realizing it. For the last few minutes, her mind was so focused on Joe that she had not realized how long it had been. She felt the direction of gravity shift to behind them and the roar of the engines and the deceleration burn and the added push of the engines on her body and she was pushed into the seat and she knew she was going to pass out…but she did not.

She closed her eyes as the ship leveled out at the last second. She felt the ship hit the ground, then suddenly lurch and seem to lag for a moment. When she opened her eyes, she wished she had passed out after all. Outside the window, she could see that the ship was spinning on the ground.

"Just what Adam was afraid of," Joe said, trying to conceal his fear. "The inflatable tire blew. I think they deflated the others just in time to keep us from falling over."

Nancy stared at him, her eyes showing the question that she voiced. "You mean the ship's on its belly?

A nod came from the paranormal investigator. "Fortunately," he said, "it looks like Commander Singh is able to use the maneuvering engines to avoid rocks, but sometimes it makes us spin worse." Truly, he was one hell of a pilot.

Sure enough, at that moment the ship seemed to lurch to the right of its direction of motion, but the ship did not spin as fast. Nancy felt sick, but luckily she had not eaten recently. She believed she would have lost it by then, anyway. A minute later, the ship had slowed enough to give better control. Gary controlled the ship with more ease. He finally began using a very weak thrust from the engines, just enough to keep the ship moving at a slow pace. They watched carefully for several minutes before a bright light several kilometers away shined in their direction. "Is that them?" Nancy asked.

Rick excitedly answered, "It must be. Take us there, Commander." Turning to Nancy, he asked, "Doctor Villareal, can you tell if we've hit the target?"

Looking at the inclines to either side of them, she answered, "We must be in Gipul Carena. I think the light was near the north end. We're really lucky. It could have taken us forever to find them.

Almost as if on cue, the flash recurred from the same location. "There it is again," Rick said. "That must be them."

As they continued moving slowly toward what Nancy believed was north, Yolanda called from the mid deck, "What's going on? Can we come back up, yet?"

Without hesitation, Rick answered, "No, not yet."

Several eerily noisy minutes went by as they slid slowly across the ice. As they approached the wreckage, they began to realize it looked similar to the ships they had seen when they turned around in the battle zone, from what they could see from such a distance. They could just make out the American flag on the side. "Do you know what this means?" It was Joe who posed the question.

Nancy looked at him, but Rick asked, "What?" just as she began moving her lips.

"It means," said Joe, "that the United States was involved in the battle we saw."

Nancy's mind spun in confusion, even more confusing thoughts racing through her mind. The question she finally posed was, "If they were hostile, then why didn't they kill us all right then?" Joe, surprisingly, remained quiet. She had her suspicions, and among them was that the boy she had grown up with not only was right all along, but suspecting more that he did not want to share.

Gary turned off the engine and let the ship slide to a stop. As they slowed in their approach, the unmistakable markings of a United States ship became plainly visible on the side of the saucer-shaped ship. Two suited beings emerged as the Diablo stopped a few yards away.

"Okay," said Rick, "you can come up now." The Spanish words that followed sounded unkind. Nancy decided it would be prudent not to voice the harsh translation.

None of them could stop talking about the fact that they may have been about to meet the first humans any of them had seen in seven months. They wasted no time entering their suits, depressurizing the crew compartment, and opening the door. Rick led the way out and the newly rescued astronauts welcomed them to the satellite with as much of an embrace as the suits would allow. The two survivors motioned that their radio was out, and Rick motioned for them to enter the Diablo. "Adam, Yolanda, Joe," he ordered, "you three go over to that ship and see what you can find. The rest of you make room for our new friends."

"Yes, sir," they all said.

Rick, always the professional, said, "We need to find out what happened, so we're going to shut you out for a few minutes so we can talk with them directly."

Adam turned away from the door for a moment while Yolanda and Joe looked at each other. "Roger," said Yolanda.

Nancy watched them leave, feeling slightly envious, but happy that Joe was doing what he wanted to do all his life. She stared for a moment longer after Rick closed the hatch, and she was the last one to remove her helmet after the compartment was repressurized.

Chapter Ten

The three scientists assigned to study the crash site carefully strode forward to the downed vessel, treading carefully on the slick ice covered with a very thin layer of dirt. Behind them, a streak of melted ice led away from the Diablo in a slightly irregular curve.

"Adam," said Yolanda, "look at the engine. Joe, you go inside and see what you can find."

"I'm sorry," said Adam after a brief moment. "I just noticed Jupiter."

Indeed, it was the first time that Joe and Yolanda had noticed the glorious site of the giant gas planet toward their left, looming like an enormous third quarter moon. The great red spot was just in the world's day side, framed by the peak of the towering ice mountains not so far away. They stopped and stared at the world with its colored bands for about a full minute before Joe said, "Come on. We still have a job to do."

As they arrived, Joe took a quick look around, knowing that Adam would spend much of his time staring at the planet that the ice world they stood upon was orbiting instead of the engine he was supposed to be checking. As he found the door and stepped toward it, the engineer's voice entered his suit saying, "One of the thrusters is melted. It looks like something came in direct contact with it."

As Joe entered the ship, he spotted what appeared to be a handwritten book. He walked over to it while Yolanda told Adam, "It sounds like it may have been fighting with that ship we boarded and was hit by some kind of direct heat weapon, or something with the same effect. Describe it."

"It's a round hole in the thrust port wall," Adam said. "Perfectly round, like melted candle wax. Wait." Joe wondered what Adam was doing during the pause. "It's malleable. Soft. A piece just broke off when I touched it."

Yolanda responded, "Don't touch anything else. Joe, what does this sound like to you?"

Still reading, Joe answered, "It sounds like it may have been a ball of plasma, but I don't know why it would still be malleable. I think I may have found out what happened, though. I've found a written log in here. It says they were part of a fleet. They ran into an enemy force. It names them as the Dahm." He stopped for a moment as a thought occurred to him. "Odd."

Joe noticed Yolanda step inside and begin moving to him as she asked, "What is odd?"

"Huh?" Joe said. "Oh, sorry, just a thought I had about something." He did not want to say it aloud, especially with Yolanda's potential reaction. "Anyway, several of them came out to fight a ship that had entered…my God. . ." Suddenly, instead of having pieces that stood side by side but would not fit together, the jigsaw now fell into place. In Joe's eyes, two plus two no longer made twenty-two.

Adam's voice was unusually eerie as he asked, "What's wrong?"

"Hold on," Joe answered. "Let me see if I can find something." Several moments passed as he ruffed through the book with Yolanda eyeing him suspiciously. A few seconds later before he finally found what he was looking for and answered, "According to this log, they were protecting a colony that's been established to produce clones to use as soldiers."

"Oh, God."

"Quiet, Adam," said Yolanda. "Joe, what does this mean?"

Joe carefully sat in the unstable chair and said, "It means that not only have we been fighting this war for so long that we've had time to establish ourselves in space, but we have technology that the general population thinks only exists in the movies, or has just recently been announced."

With a blank stare at nothing Adam said, "Well, the engines on this thing are almost identical to our own. The fuel tanks were well shielded, but they almost ruptured on impact. They're lucky the propheletyline didn't explode. There's a lot of fuel left, so they must have come from nearby."

"Ganymede," Joe said. "They must have been assigned to defend the base."

Yolanda sat beside Joe and took his hands for her own comfort. Staring at him through their face plates with her beautiful Hispanic eyes, she said "Joe, you are the one who was chosen for this mission because of your lifelong study of what we've found. You must be able to figure out what is happening."

Joe noticed Adam enter in the corner of his eye and he took a quick glance to let Yolanda know. "No," Joe said. "Something's still missing. All I don't know is where the Dahm came from and why they're here. I think the answer's in that pyramid on Mars."

Yolanda raised her arms and said, "The door? Then we go back."

"It's not that easy," Joe said. "There's more, but I'm not sure about most of it." It was not entirely true; he did not want to mention his suspicions in case Commander Newman was listening. "I'd like to go out and look at the melted thruster if that's all right with you, Doctor."

She turned to the console and said, "Go ahead. I think I may be able to figure things out in here."

"Thank you," Joe said as he began to exit the ship. Before he left, he stopped, turned, and pointed, saying, "By the way, that's the ship's log."

Yolanda turned to it and said, "I'll bring it back with me."

Adam was waiting in the doorway. He nodded and said in a voice less shaky than usual, "Let me show you the way. It really surprised me when I saw it. The closest thing I've ever seen to it is when a cigarette burns through a sheet of paper." Half a minute later, they rounded the stern of the ship. "Here it is," Adam said as he pointed to the damage.

Joe had to agree that Adam's description was accurate. The upper right port had an almost perfectly round hole one third of its size in its side and the edge of the area was warped into gentle curves that indicated heat. A triangular hole showed where Adam had broken off part of the thruster, which now lay on the ground. The other two thrusters were intact, but the landing against the cliff had created a hole in the side of the ship. "Incredible," Joe said. "Doctor Flores, when you get a chance, you may want to see this."

"That won't be necessary," came Commander Newman's voice, much to Joe's surprise. "Return to the Diablo right away."

"Roger," said Yolanda. "Let's go. Maybe they spotted the rocket." Joe suspected otherwise, but kept it to himself.

As they walked back up to the ship, they saw that the alien body—the Dahm body—had been carelessly thrown out and now lay on the ground nearby. It was not as splattered as one might have expected because of the low gravity.

Adam led the way up the ladder, followed by Joe and finally Yolanda, who carried the ship's log. Once they were in the mid deck, Commander Singh greeted them and said, "Wait here for repressurization." Yolanda closed the hatch and the barely audible hiss of air being moved back into the front section from the space lab told them that it would be safe to remove their suits in a few seconds. "Everyone's in the space lab," Rick said as he reached the airlock to the midsection of the ship. "Go ahead and take your suits off." Gary came down the ladder into the mid deck and gave a quick greeting as he followed Rick into the space lab.

Once they were all back in their cooling-ventilation garments, they entered the space lab to find the two rescued pilots sitting at the table. Captain Newman sat across from them, Nancy leaned against the wall, and Walker sat on the floor nearby. "Where's Zack?" Joe asked.

Rick looked at him and said, "He began to feel ill. He's in his bunk resting." Turning back to the two pilots, he said, "Tell them."

One of the pilots, identified as "E. Sanchez" by his name badge, began, "We were sent here to try to detain the invasion force that occupies the outer planets of our solar system. We began fighting fifty years ago, when we first went into space and discovered that their species, the Dahm, had begun setting up a base on Pluto."

Fifty years? Joe thought. That was before Yuri Gagarin. This kept getting better and better.

Sanchez continued, "Last month, a large ship approached our base on Ganymede. It took several ships to destroy it, but only we survived." Joe knew that everyone should have been surprised at the words, but a quick glance around told him that none of them were as surprised as he was. "Something hit our ship, like a fireball. We lost control and crashed here. Fortunately, our food recycling system remained operational, and we could melt the ice for water, but we had no radio. Fortunately, plants are a standard for ships and we were able to use them for survival, but they didn't last long. We were down to our last oxygen tank when you showed up." He paused, glanced downward, and continued, "Not long after, we walked outside to look for a rescue ship, and we could see lights coming from the surface of Ganymede. We realized that they were fires and explosions. The colony we had established there is gone. After that, we think they used it as a launching point for a huge fleet."

"I wonder if that had anything to do with the fleet we ran into," said Joe.

Sanchez continued, "A few hours ago, we were found by a Dahm patrol ship. As it was moving in, one of our ships appeared and chased it away. It sounds like the ship you ran into. We didn't know if our ship told our people our location or not."

Walker stared at Sanchez and said, "How did you know about that ship?"

The second pilot, O. Davison, said, "You mentioned it. We threw out the body."

With growing anxiety, Walker added, "We never mentioned it to you or told you where the body came from."

Adam became far more visibly nervous than usual. "What's going on?" he demanded.

Joe stepped forward and screamed at Rick through clenched teeth, "We've been sacrificed! The crash! The battle three years ago! You knew all along that they were here!"

"Sit down!" screamed Rick with authority.

Refusing to follow the orders of someone who had betrayed them, Joe continued, "That's why we're here! You just wanted us out of the way!"

Rick screamed, "Be silent! You have no authority over me!"

Joe's irate reply was to lunge at Rick, but the commander easily stopped him and shoved him roughly to the ground. Rick punched his lunging attacker squarely in the jaw, allowing no chance to fight back before losing consciousness.

Nancy stared in horror at Joe's unconscious form, but before she could act in his defense Sanchez and Davison both jumped up and pulled what appeared to be small rifles out of their space suits. "Sit in those chairs," said Sanchez. "Ollie, tie them up." Davison pulled out several feet of thread from a small hole in the wrist of his suit. Nancy did not want to know how strong it was.

Davison was beginning to walk to them when a gunshot suddenly rang out from the mid deck, cutting through Sanchez's shoulder and sending him to the floor, losing his gun in the process. Davison dived behind Nancy, but she threw herself forward and kicked his face, sending him to the floor where Gary kicked his gun away. Rick simply stood in place with his jaw agape as Adam and Walker both jumped him. Disarmed and outnumbered, the captain and two new arrivals held up their hands in surrender.

Gary began walking to the entry to the space lab, where Zack was standing with his gun still solidly in his hands. Obviously, he was not as ill as he had claimed. "How did you know?" the pilot asked.

"I'm a Marine," he answered. "We're trained to see, hear, and improvise. We also have to know military strategy inside and out. When that fleet let us pass through unharmed, I became suspicious. When we talked about the battle and the crash, I knew something was up. When we found these two here, I knew it was time to act."

Gary walked over to Rick and kneeled down as Nancy used the thread from Davison's suit to restrain him. "Why?" was all he could say.

Rick looked Gary straight in the eye and said, "You don't know why they're here. If they were peaceful, why didn't they just make themselves known?"

"They've tried," Joe groggily said as he began pulling himself to his feet. "If they were hostile, they would have had no problem defeating us with how advanced they must be. Why let us advance to the point where we can fight them? Or even take the chance of us stealing their technology and finding a way of neutralizing it?"

Walker had other concerns on his mind. "Take off your suit," he said to Joe. "I want to make sure you're all right after that blow you took." He looked at Sanchez. "Then I want to look at your shoulder."

While Joe complied, Adam finished tying up Sanchez and fell to the floor in relief. "What do we do now?" the engineer asked. "We can't go back."

As he was about to answer, Joe winced at Walker's touch to the back of his neck. "Does that hurt?" asked Walker.

"Like hell," Joe answered in pain. He then shifted his eyes to Adam and said, "I hesitate to say it, but going back is exactly what we have to do."

"What?" said Nancy as the others stared. Captain Singh almost took offense as the ranking officer after the mutiny; however, the parapsychology expert had the best chance of understanding the situation.

Joe winced again and glared at one of their former commander. "Back on Mars," he said, "you kept us from opening a door in that pyramid. Why?"

The mission commander looked over at the parapsychology expert with hostility, then brought himself to calmness and said, "Nobody's ever been able to get inside, or at least that's what I was told. The mission was to look for anything odd that may be a way in without letting any of you in on it." He looked at Nancy with intense hatred

Joe looked as if he wanted to slap himself silly. "Nancy, get the rock." As Nancy reached up to open her locker to retrieve her sample, Joe asked, "It's a key, isn't it? You figured if there was a key it would be by the door, but why would anyone—ow! Careful, Walker!—Why would anyone leave a key under the doormat if it's inside where it won't be reached? It was outside. Nancy found it."

"I haven't even seen it," Rick said. "I don't know if it fits or not. I only know what it's supposed to look like"

"Show him," Joe said to his long-time friend. Nancy moved the rock in front of Rick so he could see it clearly. The flight commander's face went ashen, an obvious indication them that Joe was right.

Nancy looked around and saw Yolanda sitting in the booth above Davison, staring at Joe. With a passionate eye, she said, "I can't believe it was you who figured this out." She shook her head in disbelief. "When you told me why you were on this mission, I thought you were..."

"Nuts?"

"Yes, that's it. I'm sorry, Joe. It seems that without you, we would all be—I don't know where we would be."

Nancy leaned down to the prisoners and said, "A great question. Joe, how are possible talkers usually handled back home?"

Sometimes it's like Bridget's family. Simple imprisonment. Sometimes it's more subtle. Sometimes it's more violent. Sometimes they just vanish." He looked at Rick with such intensity it made Nancy involuntarily look back off from the captive. "But nothing like this," he continued. "Why were we brought out here? What's the real mission? It looks like it's to rescue these pilots, but why a possible danger to your plot such as landing on Mars? Why Cydonia?"

Rick finally relaxed, accepting that he could do nothing. "We had to find out as much as we could about the Dahm," he said. "We know nothing about them. The idea was that you, Joe, could do that for us. You were all chosen for the very reason you've come to realize. Yes, there was a battle in space three years ago, and that was the source of everything you've figured out. I saw it, too, and they made up the drinking story. I looked into it, and I found out about the war. So, I went to NASA and told them how I felt. They created this assignment and used a cover story about the ship exploding when the propheletyline tank exploded. That's how they explained the end of communications with us." He looked at them with a hopeful hatefulness. "You were supposed to go to Ganymede afterward to help in the war."

As he returned from the hospital with an antiseptic, Walker asked, "So why all of us? Why using this method?"

Joe turned to him, then turned away to let him administer the treatment and said, "Zack talked. Yolanda talked. They knew that you knew, but they didn't know whether or not you talked. Adam received classified information. I'll bet they found out. I'll bet Bridget's still incarcerated somewhere and she finally told them what happened. I wouldn't leave the case alone. Nancy had that data her partner collected, and she's connected to me. Eventually, one of us would have started putting everything together, but any other method of handling the problem that was us either would have either been suspicious or brought attention to it. So, they took a route that wasn't either one of those, and added Cydonia as a perk. I'll bet someone tipped off the protesters at the launch that Zack or Yolanda was involved." A quick look at the mineralogist and Marine told everyone neither of the two had any idea that it could have been true.

A quick glance around told Nancy that they were all just as confused. "Why Ganymede?" she asked. "Why that colony?"

"They probably needed troops," Joe said. He sarcastically added, "Let me guess. Missing children?"

"No!" insisted Sanchez as he spun his head to Joe.

As he did, Nancy noticed something on his neck. "What's this?"

Joe jumped down to the ground so fast that Nancy jumped back. "Walker, Yolanda, come look at this," he said. Everyone stared at the almost invisibly flesh-colored piece of machinery in the side of his neck. "Can you remove it?"

"No!" all the captives screamed at once.

Without hesitation, Gary asked, "Why not?"

There were several tense moments of nervousness from the captives that seemed to draw the nerves out of Adam; for once, Nancy could not feel his essence quivering. Finally, Davison said, "We'll die if it's taken out."

"How?" Nancy was surprised that the question came from her own mouth.

Joe glared at them in the silence for nearly a minute before Davison broke down and said, "It keeps our cell structure from breaking down."

While the others wondered what it meant, Joe looked around with an anger that made them shake, wondering what he may try to do to their captives. "They're clones," he said. He pointed to the log that Yolanda had placed on the table and said, "According to your log, Ganymede was a cloning base. You were going to clone us and send those clones to fight!"

That was enough for Gary. "Secure them in here," he ordered with anger. "The rest of you get ready for takeoff. We have some refueling to do, even if there really is no rocket. We're going to use the fuel from that ship. Adam, what are that ships engines like?"

"Just like ours," the engineer answered, "and with plenty of fuel."

Gary nodded and said, "Good. We'll scrape bottom as we leave, but we're going back to Mars."

Chapter Eleven

Nothing eventful happened outside the ship on the way back to the red planet. Inside, it was different. Nancy was still nervous from her piloting encounter, but she managed to finally win a game of chess from Zack. It turned out that Rick knew about the games, movies, book, and everything else all along, so they stopped being secretive about it. A quick pass by Ganymede showed that nothing was left but ashes, and there was no sign of anyone remaining there. With the "third assignment" null and void, Rick, Davison, and Sanchez knew that any attempt at retaking the ship would be pointless, especially with Joe helping Zack on a regular basis. They also felt that they would finally be able to enter the Mars pyramid, and did not try to persuade the others not to return. Everyone was equally curious to discover what was beyond the door, while Rick felt it was part of what he had been assigned to do. They had all agreed that the solution to this great mystery of mankind could be on the other side, and Nancy's chance find led both Rick and Joe to believe that they were meant to do this.

The sun was breaking the Martian horizon as Joe and Yolanda led the way up to the pyramid shaft. Nancy carried her blue and green rock with her, held warily in her gloved hands. She wished she could feel it to make sure she did not drop it, which was why she went up third. Rick followed her to make sure she held onto it, then Walker and Adam, Sanchez and Davison, and finally the well-armed Marine. Zack had voiced his distrust of the situation, and Nancy had talked Gary into allowing him to bring weapons. Joe also carried a pistol in case something went wrong.

They reached the entrance to the shaft and looked out at the ship nearby to the right of the pyramids. It had sustained minor damage during the crash landing and takeoff from Callisto, but not enough to prevent replacing the heat shield, one thing actually done right before launch. Most of the damage had been scratches, but they decided not to take any chances. Fortunately, the path they had cleared for takeoff eight months earlier was still there and they used it to land without the need for the damaged inflatable tire. The sun glistening off the craft gave it a beautiful look. She glanced down at the ground in front of the pyramid and froze at the sight before her. In the growing sunlight, the ground was changing into a series of bluish green lights in concentric circles dotting the dull red landscape in the rising sun. "My God," came Rick's voice into her helmet.

A moment later, Nancy turned to see that she was the last to stare at Joe. From the expression on his face, he had not expected to see the sight, either. "What does it mean?" she managed to stammer out, sounding suspiciously like Adam.

In a silent, stunned shock, Joe said, "It could be one of two things. We're wrong and this isn't the key, meaning that this is the remains of what's probably an ancient ritual site. Or..." he took a breath to prepare them for the meaning of his words. "Someone wanted it to be found. I'd say that's the case."

Nancy looked down at the rock she had spotted by chance and chosen out of curiosity. It shone in the light exactly like those below, including a few that had been moved on their last visit, breaking up the edge of two of the circles. She looked out and judged that she took her rock from near where the front of the ship now sat, pointing off to their right through the edge of the design. Yolanda walked up next to her and said, "We almost destroyed it. We must have just overlooked it when we first landed here."

Nancy waited a moment in silence for the death of whatever beliefs they still held. Surely there must be something to all this, but what? Her mind wandered back to the mysterious door that waited inside.

"Let's go," Gary said. "There's only one way we may find out, and we don't know if we can go all the way back to Earth until we know for sure."

Yolanda turned and rejoined Joe a few feet inside the passage. The two of them then led the way inside, Nancy and Rick hot on their heels. They all finally stopped in the small antechamber in front of the door. "Well," said Gary, "this is it. Where's the depression?"

"Right there," Rick said as he pointed to the spherical indentation. Joe and Yolanda nodded in agreement.

Gary turned to Nancy and said, "Doctor Villareal, you have the honors."

Nancy nervously stepped up to the door and placed the rock into the depression. For a moment she thought that it had slid into something deeper before she realized it had simply slipped out, almost like two magnets repelling each other. A joke from Rick met a snarl from Zack, a constant element of the journey over the past few months since Callisto. Nancy picked up the rock and took a good look at both it and the depression and noticed for the first time a green tinge in lower part of the depression. She then found a matching green area on the rock and placed them against each other. Once she did, the rock slowly began glowing blue on the inside, the green areas blocking the inner light. As Nancy tried to pull it out, she realized it had somehow lodged itself into the wall despite no visible means. The depression began glowing in an identical manner. Gradually, the blue glow spread around the antechamber to produce an eerie aura that seemed to wriggle as if it came from a candle in a light breeze. A group of previously unseen red stones like the one Rick found in the ceiling dropped down and floated above the ground with no visible support at the level of their heads, one hitting Adam's helmet and startling him and making him swear in terror.

The sound of stone rubbing against stone could be heard through their suits, and the door slid forward slightly before stopping with a loud groan. "Help me," said Joe as he moved to pull it open. Rick came over, and together they pulled it out of the egress. As Adam and Zack helped move it to the side, Nancy let out a gasp. Yolanda and Walker both followed with almost identical reactions, and Davison muttered, "My God," under his breath.

Beyond the door was a large room with a curved wall engraved with the same hieroglyphs as there were on the side of the carved face. The downward pointing arrow was on the left, red marks visible on the white lines, looking somehow familiar to Nancy. The people came next, followed by the eye, and the outline to the far right. On the floor of the room was a drawing of a blue and green planet that bore a similarity to Nancy's rock.

"What does this mean?" asked Adam. Silence was his answer, and a glance at Joe told the engineer that even he did not know.

Joe examined the inscriptions for several minutes before he finally said, "Granite. These walls are definitely artificial. The only problem is that we have no clues as to who made them or why, but it was probably the Dahm."

Nancy turned around to leave, planning to wander off onto the planet in disappointment. As she passed through the door—open for the first time in centuries, probably millennia—into the antechamber, she froze when she saw the small red stones suspended above the ground. "That's not an arrow," she said. "Look."

When they turned around, everyone except Adam and Walker recognized the stars of the constellation Taurus made up by the red stones, one missing. Off to the side in the wall was a small, yellow cluster where the Pleades would be, and a spot in the wall seen through the head of the bull was green instead of red. Nancy turned to Joe and said, "Does this mean what I think it does?"

"If you're thinking of space travel," the paranormal investigator answered, "then I think so."

Yolanda stepped back onto the platform and looked at the hieroglyphs. She pointed at the V-shaped hieroglyph and said, "The head of the Bull." She indicated the people and said, "The Pleades." For the eye she said "Aldebaran," the star known as the eye of the bull. Finally, she said, "That's a bull. It is a map to where they've been."

Joe tried to grab his head through his helmet as he said, "Of course. Taurus is an ancient constellation, recognized by its unique V-shape. The Pleades were called the Seven Sisters. Those are seven women."

Nancy got a confused look on her face and said, "But the Pleades are on the other side of the Hyades."

"The Hyades?" asked Walker.

Nancy looked at him and explained, "The stars that make up the head of Taurus." Realization struck her face. "I'll bet they came from there and sent off exploratory missions to us and the Pleades."

"That green light could indicate the world they came from," said Joe. "They must have landed on Aldebaran next, then come here, to Mars."

Adam whined, "But Mars is a dead planet. It could never support life."

Nancy looked down at the carving on the floor. With a shock, it dawned on her. She stepped to Joe and said, "Look at the floor carving. Do you see anything familiar about it? Like, maybe, a picture you showed me once?"

Several moments went by before Davison, Sanchez, Yolanda, and Joe all noticed the same thing. "This valley," said Sanchez as he pointed to the floor carving. "This gulf."

"Jesus, Mary, and Joseph," said Yolanda. "That's what Mars would look like if it had water!"

"Maybe it did once," said Gary.

The latest deafening silence chose that moment to arrive, but it did not last long. All at once, everyone questioned what could have happened to all the water, overlapping each other so they could hear nobody but themselves despite having the same questions. A few more moments of quiet went by before the obvious came to them, but only

Joe realized exactly what had happened. He looked at Yolanda and deliberately said, "It rained for forty days and forty nights."

They all looked at him in shock, Yolanda ready to verbally lash out at him, but they all then looked at each other in silence, waiting for someone else to break it. Finally, Gary asked, "How? How could they move the water from Mars to Earth?"

Nancy and Yolanda both started to say something, and Yolanda deferred to the astrophysicist. "It doesn't seem possible," she said. "The gravitational shift of that much water being moved would affect the orbits of both planets. Maybe the entire solar system."

Sanchez leaned against the wall and said, "They have advanced technology, but we don't know how advanced. You've all seen their ships and we still can't be sure how advanced they are."

Another few minutes passed by before Adam finally decided to change the subject to something with which he felt more comfortable. "How long did it take them to get here? What kind of engine did they use?"

"It had to have been a fast, powerful engine," said Yolanda.

Gary added, "And an accurate navigation system. To travel over twenty light years so accurately is almost impossible. Even today, we could only be able to guess how on target we are, and we still have time to adjust our course. They may travel too fast to have that luxury."

Joe asked, "Is there any certain way that they could follow a straight path to their destination?"

They thought on this for several moments before Yolanda said, "They would have to have something besides the light to lock onto. Do any of you have any idea what that could possibly be?"

Only Nancy knew. "Gravity," she said in realization as she looked at Joe. "The gravitational forces are more direct. If they had an engine that used gravity as we do light, it would act like a bright line in space."

"And when they used gravity to move the water," said Yolanda, "they also used it to alter the orbits of the planets so they would stay in orbit."

Adam stepped up and said, "So why did they do that? Why did they kill themselves?"

Joe quietly said, "They didn't."

Nancy slowly turned toward him in shock, as did Sanchez and Davison. "They moved to Earth?" asked Sanchez. The thought had pushed itself into the back of Nancy's mind, only to present itself in a different way.

More shocked than anyone else, Yolanda asked, "Why?"

"Why do we have to wear ultraviolet protection?" Joe asked.

With dawning realization, Nancy answered, "There's no ozone layer."

Joe pointed in her direction and continued, "They destroyed this planet, and they—we—are doing it again. Only this time, we've lost the technology to move."

Adam asked the question on all their minds. "So, why are we fighting them?"

Davison and Sanchez stepped back into the room where Joe, Nancy, Adam, and Yolanda were. Sanchez solemnly said, "We didn't know who they were."

"We only knew they were invaders," Davison added. "They must have come to bring us back into this community of theirs."

Walker wandered back to the shaft and summed it up by saying, "We're killing our own ancestors without even knowing it."

Several seconds passed before Gary said, "Let's go. We need to refuel the Diablo. We'll only have enough to get back to Earth."

As they descended the shaft, Nancy looked at Joe and asked, "What about your Atlantis theory? How do you reconcile it?"

"It's not that hard," Joe answered. "The mid-Atlantic Ridge spans the entire side of the planet. As the water landed on top of it, it would carry the loose earth down into the ocean like a river carries silt. Plus, the waves created would flood nearly the entire world. I'll bet the ridge is where the sediment collected."

"Oh." Nancy was surprised the word came out as solidly as it did despite the fact that she said it more shakily than anything Adam had said throughout the trip.

As they all continued to descend, Rick stepped over to Joe. "How did you know?" he asked. "You were so sure that they weren't hostile. Would I be right in saying that you suspected this?"

Joe shook his head. "No," he said. "Not this. Not that we came from the stars. It's an idea that's tossed around, but I never really believed it. At least, not until I learned that their name is the Dahm."

"Now how the hell could you have figured anything out just from their name?" demanded Rick.

Now at the base of the shaft, Joe turned to Adam and asked, "What's the origin of your name?"

"The Bible," answered the engineer. "The first man, who God created."

Joe repeated, "The Bible. The first man, who God created. But where did the word come from?"

Joe looked around as they exited the shaft, causing Nancy to involuntarily react the same way. When she looked at Yolanda, she knew the Roman Catholic had the answer. "*Adahm*," she said, "was the Hebrew name for all of humanity."

All the stunned silences of the previous year were a fanatic crowd watching their team win a world championship compared to the one that ensued after this revelation. They all walked out and back to the ship, too stunned to say another word.

Chapter Twelve

The blue, green, and white orb with its light gray companion was the most beautiful sight they had seen in the past fifteen months. The eight returning astronauts cried openly when they began realizing how it seemed to be growing, wondering what kind of reception they would make for themselves when they finally made it back home. Now, less then a day remained, and most of them were anxious to return to terra firma.

Rick, however, knew how important it was to bring what they had learned into the public eye. Although the decision to put him back in command came reluctantly, everyone had finally succumbed to the idea. "Turn on the radio," he said to Gary. He then turned to Adam and Joe and said, "You're sure you've got it hooked up right?"

"Absolutely," Joe said. "I've got a ham license, and I tried to contact aliens when I was a kid. With Adam and Ollie's help the transmitter is ready." For once, Adam kept his big mouth closed.

Rick took a deep breath before motioning to Nancy. "Do it," he said as he flipped a switch on the communications console. "Let's get this over with."

Nancy began the playback of a recording that they had made on Mars using the external cameras. It described everything they had found, and the two cosmic hitchhikers, as Joe called them, described their roles. If it was wired correctly, the signal was using the solar panels as amplifiers to broadcast their message to the entire world, overriding and taking over satellite signals.

"It's working," Gary said. "I'm picking up the audio of our message on all wavelengths."

Nancy decided that there was nothing else to do but to recycle the video several times. They had agreed upon five times, long enough for most of the planet to hear about the earth-shattering event and go wherever they needed to so they could watch it, or at least hear it. Fifty-two minutes later, as the last cycle ended, Rick said, "Commander Singh, signal for landing." Gary complied, signaling to ground control that they were heading in for landing. As time continued on, they became worried as they continued to receive no response.

Joe had missed television more than anything else and Nancy was not surprised that he found a satellite transmission from an American network. He was listening to find out what the media was making of all this. "Commander," he interrupted after three hours, "you should see this."

Everyone looked at the screen, which was reporting on activities that had recently taken place surrounding the anniversary of their "deaths" as they ventured into space. NASA had decided not to pursue another deep space mission for the time being, and pictures of their mourning families appeared on the screen. The reports said that their broadcast was being reported by NASA as a hoax and their families were calling it a cruel joke.

"I can't believe this," said Adam. "I should have realized they'd be doing this."

Joe put an arm on Adam's shoulder and said, "For once, I agree with you. I, of all people, should have known."

Walker's usually upbeat aura seemed to deflate. "What do we do now?"

"We keep trying," said Rick as he returned to the mission commander's seat. "Houston," he said into his microphone, "this is Space Shuttle Diablo. We have discovered conclusive evidence that the hostile forces we have been fighting are benevolent. We will be achieving reentry into Earth's atmosphere in two hours. We are low on fuel and cannot delay. Mission control, do you read?" Several minutes went by with Rick trying different wordings and organization to make sure they knew it was not a delayed echo. With every questioning notification of their return, the answer was a deafening silence.

As Rick was beginning to try again, he abruptly stopped in mid sentence and stared out to the side. Nancy followed with her eyes to see a group of small ships approaching their position. A moment later, a voice on the radio said, "Identify yourselves immediately or be destroyed."

"This is the space shuttle Diablo, Commander Richard Newman in command."

"Negative," the pilot said. "Diablo disappeared over one year ago. We also read ten life forms. There were only eight on Diablo. This is your final warning. Identify yourselves immediately!"

Rick anxiously said, "We picked up two survivors of a war. They are human. They can answer all questions if you will let us land!"

Sanchez quickly floated to the console and said, "Earth Defense Fleet, you are required to let us land under the Patterson Communications Law."

After ever so brief pause, the now highly irritated voice demanded, "Who the hell is this?"

Sanchez answered, "This is Flight Commander Edward Sanchez, serial number SX67E8S." He emphasized the first two letters. "You are ordered to verify my identification."

A moment went by. "Who else is in there with you?" the incoming pilot asked.

Davison moved up and said, "Lieutenant Oliver Davison, serial number SX69K1F."

On their enhanced radio, they heard the approaching captain say on another frequency, "Houston, did you get that?"

"Affirmative," said another voice. "Hold for verification, but prepare to move in. Be ready to target the fuel tanks."

With a start, Adam whispered, "The propheletyline." It made sense. What better to destroy unwelcome visitors than by causing the entire structure to rupture?

The group inside the larger ship relaxed for the moment. "What do we do now?" asked Nancy.

"We wait." It was not like Rick to make such statements, but there was nothing else to do. Yolanda responded to the ensuing silence by putting an arm on Adam's shoulder.

One minute later, the voice identified as Houston said, "Alpha squadron, do not attack. Escort the ship to the primary landing area."

As the crew collectively released their breaths, Joe wondered, "'Primary landing area'? Why do I get the feeling that's bad news?"

Rick looked back at him and said, "It depends on how you want to look at it. I'm assuming if they're referring to where spaceships land, it's in Nevada."

The groan from Joe's mouth made them wonder where they were headed. Nancy knew, and it made her feel no better.

They sat in silence as the ship cooled enough to safely open the access hatch leading to the ground they now dreaded to walk down the stairwell toward. After the hour was finished, they quietly rose and prepared to open the hatch to leave. A stairwell had been brought out, much to Joe's surprise but not to the others; he later realized that such a landing area would have to be prepared for such an event.

"What do you think they'll do?" asked Adam, fear sweeping through his voice.

Joe answered, "Ollie, Eddie, I don't think you'll have much to worry about. Rick, once this is explained I think they'll understand that you acted this way because of our actions. As for the rest of us, we'll have to prove our story and hope they believe it."

Rick nodded as Nancy put her head on Joe's shoulder. "They're ready," the flight commander said as he motioned to the door leading outside.

Joe nodded and said, "We're ready, too." The others all nodded in agreement.

Rick turned the wheel and opened the hatch. He led the way onto the stairwell, followed by Eddie and Ollie, then Gary, Nancy, Joe, Yolanda, Adam, Walker, and finally Zack. Each of them carried the rocks they had picked up in a specimen jar, including Nancy, who had found it on the ground when she later returned to the pyramid.

As they walked down, they looked at the hundreds of armed guards around and were certain they would not be able to tell their tale. They prepared to be arrested as they arrived at the bottom, but much to their surprise the general saluted and all the surrounding troops followed suit. Nancy took a quick glance behind her at the others. Adam was wondering what was about to happen, Nancy saw it was going to be good.

The general walked up to Rick and saluted. Rick returned the salute and acknowledged the general's rank by the name Williams. The officer glared at him and said, "Welcome back, Commander. I'm surprised to be talking with you. Nobody expected to ever hear from you again."

Rick answered, "To be honest, it was Lieutenant Knight who allowed these discoveries by an act of mutiny that I later agreed was in humanity's best interest because of our discoveries. Mister Rommel and Doctor Villareal were the ones who figured everything out, with some help from Doctor Flores and Doctor Licht. Mister McCrone is responsible for getting us back safely."

General Williams stepped to the two rescued pilots, and they saluted each other. "From the Seed Experiment, I understand."

"Yes, sir," said Sanchez. They recognized the term "Seed Experiment" as the name Eddie and Ollie gave for the cloning project on Ganymede.

The general explained, "You should know that the Dahm didn't destroy the Ganymede station. They were invading it, and rather than let it fall into their hands the decision was made to destroy it." To the entire group, he said, "That's how they worked. They invaded, but they never tried to kill anything but clones unless they had to." He finally stepped over to Nancy. "I understand you found the key to the door."

"Yes, sir." She handed him her container.

He looked at it for several moments for great interest, then asked, "Do you know how it works?"

Nancy shook her head. "No," she said, "but it has light reflecting and enhancing qualities. I doubt if we could even begin to understand it. It lodged itself in a crevice. This is one of the ones from the outermost circle outside the pyramid."

"And you entered the hidden chamber with it. Absolutely astounding. The way that they were laid out on the ground was the tip-off and we never discovered it. I only wish you could have shown us the room you mentioned." He thought for a moment, staring at Nancy's specimen. "I knew something was up," he continued. "There had to be some reason why they never just attacked with all their superior technology. We didn't have any way of stopping them, but they never attacked with everything they had. They told us, but we didn't believe them. We thought it was some kind of trick. We finally decided that they wanted to make us all slaves, but they still must have had some technology that would have made us helpless to stop them. We just didn't have anything to go on except their word, which we didn't trust." He looked at them all. "You did the world a great service. The President has told the United Nations Security Council everything they didn't know before, and they're already working on a resolution to end the secrecy. The war is over because of you. I've never been so happy to give anyone a salute as I salute you." As he did, the entire military force present also saluted. Afterward, everyone suddenly began cheering and thrusting their rifles into the air with one hand. The biggest party in the history of mankind was about to begin. Nancy only wondered what the food would be; anything would be good after living off recycled crap for over a year.

In the months that came, the entire crew received almost every commendation the world could award them. Even the Dahm gave them awards for courage, ingenuity, and insight. The discoveries stunned the world. There was some violence, mostly from those who protested the launch and staunch Christian activists, but most of the reaction was tearful for every possible reason. Most importantly, the war was over. Within two years, the beings who called themselves mankind rejoined the Dahm and ventured back into space.

Epilogue

Joe stared out the window at the Dahm homeworld. They had discovered it after several years of searching, guided by the map in the Mars pyramid. A yellow sphere mottled by dark patches, a desert world that held the origins of Dahm civilization. Now, nothing survived upon its surface.

He turned back to the table and examined the tablet, the Rosetta Stone of Dahm civilization. Just like the Greek, Demotic, and hieroglyphic of the ancient Egyptian tablet, this over two hundred thousand years old manuscript, contained ancient, forgotten Dahm lettering and another, similar script found on Mars had already been decoded by several top authorities on the subject. To everyone's surprise, it told where they established three more lost Dahm colonies. He glazed over the find he had been most fortunate to make. He proudly remembered how he recognized the usage of false tombs in Egypt, leading to the discovery of a recorded history within the Mars monument and below a structure on the world below that Nancy had nicknamed the Dahm Eiffel Tower.

The door opened and Nancy entered with a child of about six. "Hi, sweetheart," Joe said as he rose to kiss his wife of eight years. He kneeled down to his daughter. "And how's my sweet Jesse today?"

"Fine, Daddy," she said.

Nancy looked at her husband with a smile. "We just came back from Calra." It was what they believed to be one of the oldest cities. "They've discovered dried up underground springs, and a colony ship is going to try to set up here. Every archeologist in the Dahm civilization wants in, and a few humans, too."

Joe's eyes lit up as he said, "Wonderful! Did you have fun?"

Jesse's face beamed as she said, "It was great! I saw all sorts of stuff!" She began listing off things to fast for Joe to take in all at once, just like always.

"Great," said Joe. "Now, it's time for you to go to bed. Go get ready and I'll be right there to tuck you in."

Jesse said, "Okay, Daddy," as she kissed his cheek and ran off to her bedroom.

Joe was taken aback and simply said, "Wow. I don't know if she'll get much sleep tonight."

"She won't?" Nancy asked. "I don't think I will. They're making a new discovery every few minutes. They almost decided not to turn on the hydrizers."

Joe thought about the moisture developing machines and said, "With what we've seen over the last ten years, I don't think that a simple thing like an ocean would stop them." He turned to the couch, as they had named the soft protrusion from the wall, and sat upon it. "I heard from Adam and Bridget today. He's thrilled. He's found a way to increase engine output by two percent. That means every light year will take fifteen hours less."

"Wonderful," Nancy said as she lay down on the couch, putting the back of her head on Joe's lap. "I still can't believe we're responsible for this. All I did was pick up a rock, and the entire universe changes on me." She looked at the remains of the key encased against the wall, and the whole one beside it made especially for her. "Have you heard from any of the others?"

"I have," Joe answered. "I was talking with Yolanda right after you left earlier. She just got her certification from a master on Aldebaran and she's been made chief science officer on Gary's ship."

Nancy stayed still, looking directly upward. "I can't believe they're going to explore a new territory," she said. "Alpha Centauri. It's hard to believe they never went there in the last twelve thousand years. If the Mars crisis had never happened, they would have." She sighed. "I can't believe Gary's a captain on an exploratory mission." She began to laugh. "I really can't believe Yolanda married a Dahm priest!" Joe joined her in laughter. "Amazing, isn't it?"

"Which?" Joe asked. "That Yolanda married a priest, or that the Dahm have a religion?"

Nancy laughed and said, "That we're famous throughout every star system. That we're going to go down in history as two of the people who were responsible for the reunion between our peoples. That we've become legends." She smiled to herself and let it sink in further.

Joe waited a moment for the full impact of her words and said, "Zack's requested an assignment on Gary's ship, too. I'm surprised they haven't tried to get us on the mission."

"We're just as important here," Nancy said. "They know what to do. You taught them well. I'm just sorry Zack felt so disillusioned by our journey together." She rose and went to the bookshelf, where she saw Rick's autobiography on top. "We'll have plenty of time to read this before we arrive. Do you think Walker will write a book?"

Joe rose and moved back to the table, taking a quick glance over the tablet. "Not soon," he said. "He's too busy being Earth's leading expert on Dahm physiology. I don't think he'll ever be able to leave the planet again. I just wonder why Rick decided to stay on Earth. I agree that Florida's nice, but he's an explorer."

They both thought for a moment. "It doesn't matter," Nancy said. "After fifteen months in space, none of us wanted to leave. But duty calls. I'll be saying good night to Jesse."

"I'll be in there in a moment," Joe answered. After Nancy left, he walked back to the window to look at the other three ships set to go with them to try to find the other three lost branches of Dahm civilization. Truly, man's mistake had cost the Dahm greatly; the financial burdens that war caused had force the Dahm to leave, letting the

A-Dahm—the name that had been assigned to the Dahm group that settled on Mars—fend for themselves.

His eyes moved down to the planet as the hydrizers began to work their magic on the planet's surface. The first hint of clouds could be seen beginning to form, and within days rain would strike the surface for the first time in centuries, perhaps millennia. It was a new beginning for the dead world.

Nancy rejoined him as the ships turned in preparation to leave. After a moment, the planet disappeared as the ship thrust itself into gravitic drive, no sign of it being felt inside. Even after seven years, it still startled him. He gave a kiss to his wife, and went to tell his daughter goodnight. All night long, he had dreams of the repopulating of the Dahm homeworld.

About the Author

W.G. Walters is 30 years old and lives in Houston, Texas. This is his first novel.

Printed in the United States
1540100005B/150